WAYNE STINNETT

& KIMBERLI A. BINDSCHATEL

VIGILANT CHARITY

A CHARITY STYLES NOVEL

Caribbean Thriller Series

Volume 5

2019

Published by DOWN ISLAND PRESS, LLC, 2019
Beaufort, SC

Library of Congress cataloging-in-publication Data
Stinnett, Wayne
Vigilant Charity/Wayne Stinnett
Vigilant Charity/Kimberli A. Bindschatel
p. cm. - (A Charity Styles novel)

ISBN-13: 978-1-7339351-0-4
ISBN-10: 1-7339351-0-X

Cover photograph by Serge Skiba
Graphics by Wicked Good Book Covers
Edited by The Write Touch
Final Proofreading by Donna Rich
Interior Design by Ampersand Book Designs

This is a work of fiction. Names, characters, and incidents are either the product of the author's imagination or are used fictitiously. Any resemblance to actual persons, living or dead, businesses, companies, events, or locales is entirely coincidental. Most of the locations herein are also fictional or are used fictitiously. However, we take great pains to depict the location and description of the many well-known islands, locales, beaches, reefs, bars, and restaurants throughout the Florida Keys and the Caribbean to the best of our ability.

FOREWORD

From Kimberli

A big thank you to Wayne for trusting me to step in and further develop this vibrant character he's created. It's a great honor. He felt having a woman help with the writing would bring more depth to the character. I have no idea why he chose me; I'm such a tomboy. Ha! But the more I got to know Charity, the more I saw all the things we have in common—mainly, a desire for justice.

There's an old rule of storytelling: create a fantastic character, then put her in a position that pushes her to the brink. As Wayne and I shot ideas around, one situation stood out. I knew it was the way to really show how far Charity has come. I hope you enjoy reading this story as much as we enjoyed inventing it.

From Wayne

I met Kimberli at the annual Novelists, Inc conference last year in Florida. I already knew a little about her and had read a couple of her books. On every one of my books' pages on Amazon, right at the top was an ad for Kimberli's Poppy McVie series. I wanted to find out how to do that. She and I talked for a while and I learned that she and her husband were avid sailors on the Great Lakes.

That's when an idea popped into my head, and having no filter, I blurted out, "What would happen if Jesse and Poppy met?" Ideas started flying back and forth and I knew instantly that we were on to something.

Poppy and Jesse did meet in my Rising Charity and Kimberli's Dolphin Spirit, and that first encounter was hilarious. You'll have to read that firsthand and put the two books side by side to see what I mean. Even though the action and dialogue is the same in both books, the scene was totally different, due to Jesse's and Poppy's differing view points.

I'd been looking for someone to co-write the Charity series with me for a couple of years. I'd helped Charity evolve as much as I could. But being a man, I found writing from a woman's perspective one of the hardest things I've ever done. The action scenes were no problem but getting inside her head was the difficult part. So, I approached Kimberli about taking on a new project. And now you hold it in your hands. I hope you'll enjoy reading this new side of Charity. She's still a force to be reckoned with, no doubt about it. But she is starting to develop in ways I never could have imagined, much less write.

Many thanks to our team of beta readers, Dana Vilhen, Katy McKnight, Debbie Kocol, Thomas Crisp, Ron Ramey, Torrey Neill, Mike Ramsey, Alan Fader, Charles Höfbauer, John Trainor, David Parsons, Drew Mutch, Deg Priest, Glen Hibbert, and Debbie Cross, for helping to polish up the manuscript. We'd also like to give our appreciation to those who followed: editor Marsha Zinberg, final proofreader Donna Rich, interior designer Colleen Sheehan, cover creator Shayne Rutherford, and audio narrator Nick Sullivan. Without all these people, experts in their fields, this story would be far less entertaining. Thank you.

This book is dedicated to the 1000+
members of Novelists, Inc.
Only through our involvement with
NINC, could Kimberli and I have
met and talked about "what if" in a
setting that really fosters creativity.

*"As long as we remain vigilant at building
our internal abundance—an abundance
of integrity, an abundance of forgiveness, an
abundance of service, an abundance
of love—then external lack is bound to be temporary."*

- Marianne Williamson

If you'd like to receive my newsletter,
please sign up on my website:

WWW.WAYNESTINNETT.COM.

Every two weeks, I'll bring you insights into my private life and writing habits, with updates on what I'm working on, special deals I hear about, and new books by other authors that I'm reading.

The Charity Styles Caribbean Thriller Series

Merciless Charity
Ruthless Charity
Reckless Charity
Enduring Charity
Vigilant Charity

The Jesse McDermitt Caribbean Adventure Series

Fallen Out
Fallen Palm
Fallen Hunter
Fallen Pride
Fallen Mangrove
Fallen King
Fallen Honor
Fallen Tide
Fallen Angel
Fallen Hero
Rising Storm
Rising Fury
Rising Force
Rising Charity
Rising Water

THE GASPAR'S REVENGE SHIP'S STORE IS OPEN.

There, you can purchase all kinds of swag related to my books. You can find it at

WWW.GASPARS-REVENGE.COM

MAP

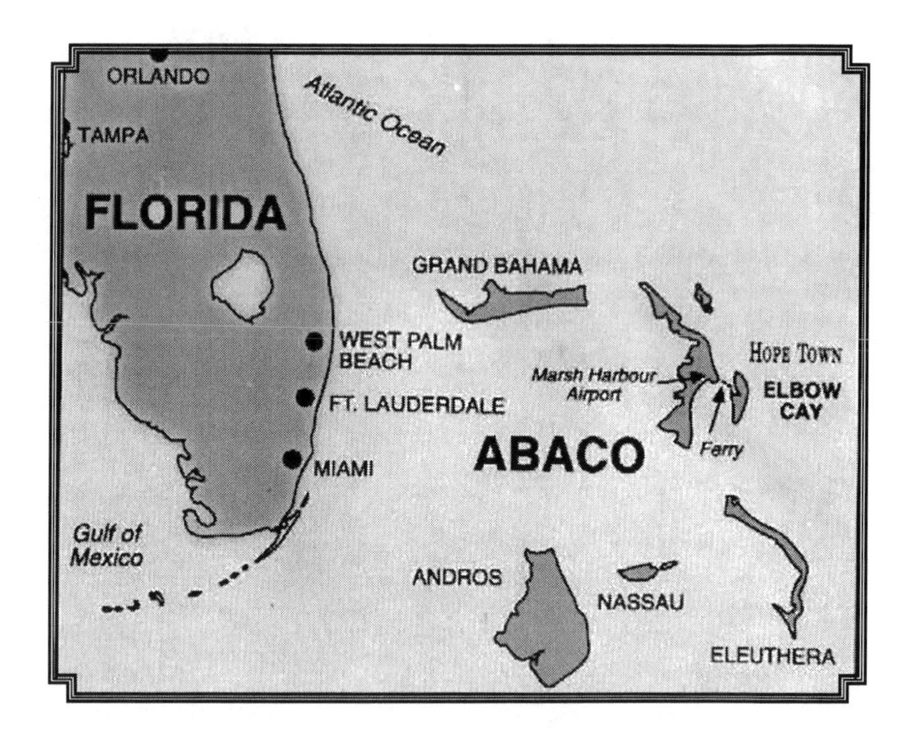
ORLANDO
TAMPA
Atlantic Ocean
FLORIDA
GRAND BAHAMA
WEST PALM
BEACH
FT. LAUDERDALE
MIAMI
Hope Town
Marsh Harbour
Airport
ELBOW
CAY
Ferry
ABACO
Gulf of
Mexico
ANDROS
NASSAU
ELEUTHERA

Abaco

CHAPTER ONE

As it knifed through the waves, the steady swish of the boat's bow wave whispered like a lullaby. It was the only sound that could be heard. Even the sails were silent; filled by the consistent southeasterly trade winds, there was no luff or chatter. The sun was bright, warm, and welcoming, like the embrace of a dear friend.

Returning to the tranquil waters of The Bahamas was bittersweet for Charity. It had been a long time since Victor had been killed in Nassau, but the memories of their time together still lingered as if they had just happened yesterday. He'd been the only man Charity had truly loved.

She and Victor had spent months anchored in secluded coves all up and down the vast island chain. She hadn't been sure how she would feel sailing these waters again, but now that she'd returned, in some ways, it felt like coming home.

Of all the places she'd sailed, nothing compared to the crystal blue waters of The Bahamas. She felt as if she were floating on liquid gemstones—sapphires, aquama-

rines, deep, dark green emeralds. Charity didn't much care for jewelry. The idea of adorning herself with dangling, shiny baubles denoting wealth seemed ridiculous to her, but here, as *Wind Dancer* glided along the surface, she considered herself as rich and comfortable as any queen.

Except for around Nassau. She wasn't ready to go near there. Too much heartache. She raised her face toward the sun and closed her eyes, drawing in a breath of the warm, salt air, and tried not to think about Victor and how he'd died. That was in the past. She couldn't bring him back.

Somehow, amid the pain, fate had given her Moana and Fiona, two captives of a diabolical couple who used them as pawns in their schemes of robbery and murder. Being able to give them new lives had helped to heal the sorrow of losing Victor. The moment Moana had reunited with her family in French Polynesia—to see her eyes come alive, as if she were able to breathe again—had brought Charity a joy she'd never experienced before. And then again, when Fiona had confided, under a moonlit sky as she and Charity gazed at the stars from *Wind Dancer's* cockpit, that she'd fallen in love, that she was ready to settle down. Charity had gladly spun the wheel to starboard, turned the boat around, back to Brisbane, Australia, and dropped her at the young man's doorstep.

To see those young women blossom, to let go of the anger and fear they'd carried with them for so long,

to finally move on to live normal lives, was inspiring. From the moment she'd met them, she knew she had to help. And she had. Charity's loss and need to mend had brought happy endings for both of those young women. Something good had come of Victor's death. Of all the jobs she'd done, none were as satisfying. She'd hang on to that. In the end, she'd made a difference. Victor would be proud.

She knew Jesse was. He'd joined her aboard *Wind Dancer* for the three-month cruise from California to the Caribbean. Sure, she could have sailed *Dancer* on her own, but she and Jesse both had a lot to sort out, and over the years they'd become confidantes to one another.

Jesse McDermitt, her best friend, had just come off of a fourteen-month bender when they'd started the cruise. His behavior was either some kind of mid-life crisis, or a juvenile reaction to finding and losing Savannah again, she wasn't sure which. He'd conveniently glossed over those painful months in their conversations. But she'd heard the stories over the nets. Perhaps he was ashamed. He'd needed the time to think, to refresh.

Charity had some demons of her own to exorcise. Sometimes they came to her, late at night as she slept under the stars. On those nights, her sleep was anything but peaceful, as she battled them back into submission. It had been a while since their last visit, but she knew she was still a work in progress.

As she and Jesse had sat in the cockpit, sharing experiences and sunsets along the way, Charity learned

a new perspective. At first, she'd worried that maybe they'd lapse into a fling. Deep down, she could admit to herself that she loved Jesse. But their friendship meant so much more to her.

Upon setting foot onto *Wind Dancer's* deck, he'd declared himself celibate. *A self-induced dry spell*, he'd called it. A good thing, because, on at least three different nights, she'd been tempted to throw her own vow to the wind. But she knew that everything would be different then, and she felt sure he thought that as well. It was difficult to ignore physical attraction, she knew that. Any notion of yanking his shorts down and blowing his mind would simply have to remain a private fantasy.

Their conversations had mostly centered around the new chapter in their lives. Charity was convinced she had to find a different purpose and was relieved to find that Jesse had come to the same realization. When he'd admitted to her that he needed a new direction, something to believe in, she'd told him of her similar thoughts. It felt as if a weight had been lifted from her shoulders. Together, they'd accepted contract employment with Armstrong Research's new Mobile Expeditionary Division.

Right now, Jesse was aboard *Ambrosia*, Armstrong's primary research vessel. He was training to dive the submersible and getting his requisite sea time for an Unlimited Master's license. That would enable him to captain the 199-foot mega-yacht turned research vessel, as a backup to the current captain.

Charity was between assignments at the moment, having spent several months aboard *Ambrosia* with other new operators, learning more about how Armstrong's operation worked and who the major players were. Many members of the board of directors had made personal visits to meet the new crew members. Interacting with all those people had felt like a sort of culture shock. So, she'd decided to continue on to The Bahamas, to see if she could make peace with Victor's ghost.

After hours upon hours of talking with Jesse, time she'd cherished, Charity enjoyed the silence. She'd always imagined the soothing sounds of the sea, the gentle waves lapping against the hull, were like those a baby hears in the womb—a slow, gentle whoosh... whoosh...whoosh that comforted the soul. They were the sounds of home, love, security.

Maybe that's why she loved sailing so much. She needed it. The swish of the bow wave, the tink-tink of the spare halyard lightly tapping the mast—slackened ever so slightly by the wind-loaded curve of the mast, the subtle twang of the rigging as the bow cut through the waves, the gentle rise and fall of the stern in a rhythm as ancient as the Earth herself. These were the sounds and motions Charity's soul required.

It was no wonder sailors became addicted to the sea. The feel of the wheel in her hands, steady on the rudder as *Wind Dancer* moved through the water at a pace set by the wind and the waves, was all she needed for her to understand what really mattered. Living in the moment,

in tune with nature, was the way to truly find peace. And that was what she intended to do. At least until she got a message from her new employer.

With the warm sun on her face, she decided to head north, into the Sea of Abaco. She had nowhere in particular to go and all the time to get there, but something drew her in that direction.

She'd find a nice spot to anchor for a week or two or maybe three, and just do whatever she felt like doing. The teak rails needed to be oiled and the sails checked. But she could do that whenever she wanted to.

Maybe she'd find a place to do some free diving. Or not. After years of military service, working for the Miami-Dade P.D., and then Homeland Security, she had no commitments. Even though she wouldn't trade the time she had with Victor for anything, they'd made her feel tied down. Now, her time was finally her own. She was free as a bird.

So why did she feel restless?

Perhaps once she found a place to anchor for a while, she'd feel more settled, and the Sea of Abaco was a world-class sailing destination. Because the barrier islands took the brunt of what the Atlantic served up, they created calm, protected waters, with hundreds of little coves to anchor in, and coral heads teeming with life.

Fortunately, it wasn't high cruising season; most of the yachties had gone back home to jobs and school, so finding a nice, private spot all to herself wouldn't be im-

possible. She'd heard about an anchorage on the northeast side of Nunjack Cay, a two-day sail from her present location, where sharks and rays swarmed around swimmers, begging for food. She didn't think feeding wildlife was a good idea, but why not check it out? That was as good a destination as any. And with a fifteen-knot southeasterly, it would be a nice, easy run.

At lunchtime, five miles south of Little Harbor, Charity flipped on the autopilot settings and headed down below to make a tuna sandwich. She glanced at her chart plotter. She'd need to find a spot to drop the hook to spend the night. As she scanned the options, a blip on the Automatic Identification System caught her eye. In a cove off Lynyard Cay, just to the north of her current position, the AIS identified *Sea Biscuit*, lying at anchor. It was Savannah Richmond and her daughter, Florence.

The thought of seeing them again, especially Flo, made Charity smile. She climbed back up to the cockpit, reset her course, and an unexpected excitement came over her. The last time they'd met up, they'd spent the day talking, enjoying a leisurely outing together, and Charity had felt like she'd finally made a friend.

Then those men had come, with their threats. Charity had taken care of them; what was left of the turd-fondlers was now at the bottom of a 600-foot blue hole, crabs picking at their bones. They'd never bother another soul and she hadn't given the incident another thought.

Now, she wondered how Savannah had handled what had happened. And Flo. A little girl shouldn't have to experience something like that.

Flo had been playing all day, diving off the rock cliff, looking for treasure, all smiles and exuberant innocence—the things a little girl is supposed to be doing, not fending off creepy men.

A knot started to form in Charity's gut. When did it happen? When was innocence lost? For her, it had been when, already motherless, her father had died unexpectedly while she was away at college and she had to face the truth—that she was on her own.

The world had come crashing down around her again, just a few years later, when the towers in New York had fallen. She was at the top of her game, coming off a bronze medal in the Sydney Olympics. Then everything changed. Nothing would ever be the same after that. The funny thing was, she knew it in an instant. Despite all those sayings about slowly growing older and wiser, for Charity, it had happened in a matter of seconds. She'd gone from being a young lady with a promising career in competitive swimming to a patriot bent on vengeance. From that moment on, her entire adult life had been an adrenaline-pumped, full-throttle rush, like a never-ending scream ride at an amusement park.

It was time to step off.

Some time with Savannah and Flo was exactly what she needed. A chance to experience a normal life—if

only for a little while. Charity was a loner. That's how it was meant to be. But over the last five years, Savannah had been as close to a real "girl" friend as Charity had ever had, even though they'd only spent a few days together. The question was, after what had happened at the blue hole, did Savannah feel the same way?

As Charity eased the sheets and turned to the northwest, *Wind Dancer* glided through Little Harbor Cut with the lighthouse off her port side. Charity hauled the sails back in to a broad reach as she headed north. Lynyard Cay was on her starboard side and the anchorage straight ahead. Through her binoculars, she spotted *Sea Biscuit*, tucked in a little cove, as peaceful as could be.

There it was again. A fluttering in her stomach. A little jitter of excitement.

Maybe it was some bad tuna, she thought. *Oh, who are you kidding?* She wanted to run and jump and dive in the water. Romp and giggle. She wanted to see that little girl smile, a real smile. She wanted to be with someone she didn't have to be on her guard against. She wanted to play. And it felt good to want those things. Even after all she'd been through.

For a one-mile stretch, she fidgeted in the cockpit, until finally she fired up the engine, doused the sails, and headed straight for the cove.

CHAPTER TWO

When she saw Savannah at the stern of *Sea Biscuit*, she waved and hollered "Ahoy!"

Savannah hesitated before waving back. Certainly, she recognized Charity and *Wind Dancer*. Was something wrong? Where was Flo? Charity scanned the water. Not swimming nearby. She caught herself. This level of paranoia wasn't normal. She needed to work on that.

She eased into the cove, chose a spot close to *Sea Biscuit*, released the anchor, then backed down on it until she was sure it was secure. Then she killed the engine.

In double time, she ducked below, secured her hatches, locked the boat up tight, and was in her dinghy, zooming across the water.

"It's so nice to see you. How have you been? How's Flo? Where is she?" The words came tumbling out as she cut the engine and neared the boat.

Have I lost my mind? Charity thought. *I'm as giddy as a schoolgirl.*

Woden, Savannah's Rottweiler, stood at her side, staring at Charity, a warning in his brown eyes. It was unnerving. He had to have been at least 120 pounds. Charity had faced many foes, but unarmed, she wasn't sure how she'd handle a dog like that if she ever had to. She'd mastered Krav Maga, an Israeli combat fighting technique where one manipulated the human body by understanding the limits of human anatomy. She had taken down men twice her size. But with a dog, all bets were off.

Savannah gave her a polite smile. "We're well. It's good to see you, too." She didn't offer for Charity to come aboard.

The air left Charity's lungs with a slow, disappointing fizz. After she'd killed those men, she and Savannah had talked all night, but then, in the morning, Savannah had left the anchorage without a goodbye. Was she afraid of Charity now?

"I, ah, just got back and I saw you on AIS. I thought maybe we could catch up."

A smile formed on Savannah's lips, as though she had just realized who Charity was. "Of course, of course. C'mon aboard." To Woden, she softly said, "It's all right." She stepped down to the swim platform, took hold of the dinghy's painter, and tied it to a cleat. Over her shoulder, she yelled, "Flo, come out and say hello."

As Charity climbed out of the dinghy and stood up on the swim platform, Flo came to the rail. "Charity!"

Charity raced up the ladder and threw her arms open wide. Flo slammed into her, wrapping her little arms around her waist. Charity held on, leaning down and burying her face in the girl's hair. She smelled like sunshine.

Woden's gaze locked on them. Savannah came up behind them and ordered the dog inside.

Flo squirmed from Charity's embrace and looked up at her with bright eyes. "Will you teach me to swim? Please, will you?"

"Swim?" Charity looked to Savannah, confused. "You already know how to swim."

"It's all she talks about, learning to swim like you." She tapped Flo on the shoulder. "Let's not pester Charity while she's here."

Flo's smile turned into a pouty frown.

Savannah went on. "I gave her a biography assignment. She was to research a famous person and for whatever reason, she Googled your name." There was something about her posture. Stiff, rigid. She was uncomfortable. "We didn't know you'd won a bronze medal at the Olympics."

"What do you mean, an assignment?" Charity asked, gracefully avoiding the compliment.

"We've decided to stay on the boat, so she's homeschooled. It's a typical fourth grade assignment."

"Boat schooled, Mom."

Charity looked at Flo, with her tiny legs and arms and that pixie face. "You're not old enough to go to school."

"I'm ten," she said, as proud as could be.

Charity's eyes met Savannah's. "Can't be. Where did the time go?"

"I know. I can't believe it either." Savannah turned, gesturing for Charity to follow. "C'mon out of the sun."

They entered the salon in the main cabin and Flo disappeared forward. The massive Rottweiler was curled up in the corner.

Savannah headed toward the refrigerator. "Have a seat. Iced tea?"

"Sure, thank you," Charity said, easing onto the white leather settee. She glanced around, taking in the interior of the vessel. She'd been aboard *Sea Biscuit*, but never inside. "Your boat is gorgeous. The woodwork is stunning." It was a 1983 Grand Banks 49 Classic. An older vessel, but it had been completely refitted with modern equipment and all new leather upholstery. The helm instruments rivaled *Wind Dancer's*. "I had no idea."

Savannah set the glass of tea on the table in front of her. "Yeah, I've got some surprises up my sleeve, too."

Her comment felt like a stab. Charity shrank a little. "Listen, I'm really sorry about lying to you that day. But it was my job, you know. I was traveling undercover."

Flo bounded up the stairs from her cabin into the room. She'd changed into her swimsuit. "Will you teach me to swim now?" Her little face glowed with anticipation.

"Well, I—"

Savannah shooed her away. "Flo, what did I say about pestering?"

Flo planted her feet. Her expression didn't change. She was one determined young lady.

"Charity just got here. Give her a minute to relax. Why don't you go get your laptop and we'll show her your research paper?"

That seemed to pacify her. Off she went, in search of her laptop.

"She's at that age, you know," Savannah said as she plopped onto the settee across from Charity. "The age when she needs to start interacting with more kids her own age. I've been doing some research of my own, looking for others in the cruising community who are in the same situation. I headed back here from Turks and Caicos hoping to connect with more cruisers with kids. Next week, we're meeting up with a family in Hope Town. I'm hoping it'll work out."

"I'm sure it will," Charity said, nodding reassurance. "She's a great kid."

Charity thought again of Victor and their plans to cruise together. They'd never talked about kids. Would he have wanted them? It didn't matter. Charity wasn't meant to be a mother. She knew that. But what if things had been different? If she could go back, make different choices, what would her life be like now? Would she be baking cookies, or driving her own daughter back and forth to soccer practice? Or living on a boat, looking for other families with kids the same age?

Flo reappeared with a laptop in her hands. She sat down next to Charity, snuggling up to her. "See." She flipped open the laptop. "I learned all about you, how you swam in the Olympics with a special innovative technique and you won the bronze medal." She gleamed with pride, as if simply knowing Charity was reason to strut about. "That must have been *so-o-o-o-o* cool."

"It was," Charity said. A smile snuck up on her. "It really was." All the joy and pride she'd felt that day was reflected in Flo's face right now. She hadn't felt that way in a long, long time. Proud.

Assassinating enemy combatants didn't quite give her the same warm, fuzzy feelings as she'd had standing on that podium, the U.S. flag flown in her honor. She'd worked hard for so many years to accomplish her dream. She'd already started training for the '04 games to be held in Athens, the city where the Olympics began. At the time, she'd had no greater goal.

"It really was so cool," Charity said again, grinning. Suddenly she wanted Flo to have that kind of experience, to feel that kind of joy. "You could do it too, if you set your mind to it."

Flo's eyes grew wide. "Will you teach me?"

"Flo!" Savannah shook her head, exasperated.

"It's all right," Charity told her. "If you don't mind. I'd really like to."

"Yipppeeeee!" Flo leapt to her feet, then up onto the settee. "Yipppeeeee!" She jumped up and down.

Woden raised his massive head, quickly assessed the situation, then laid his head back down on crossed legs.

"I was about your age when I started training," Charity said. "But it was hard work. It'll take a lot of practice."

Her head bobbed up and down. "I can do it. Practice, practice, practice. Right, Mom?" She jumped off the settee and twirled around.

Savannah glanced at the clock on the wall.

Charity recognized what that meant. "I tell you what," she told Flo. "We'll get started first thing in the morning."

Her face fell. "But I'm ready now."

"Flo," Savannah warned.

Flo's eyes flitted to Savannah and back. "First thing in the morning. I'll be ready. Bright-eyed and bushy-tailed. That's what my grandma always says." She shook her little fanny like she had a bushy tail.

"All right," Savannah told her. "Charity and I would like some time to talk. Why don't you go get ready for bed and work on your spelling lesson?"

"But Mom—"

"No buts. It's almost nine o'clock. Early to bed so you get a good night's sleep and are ready to work with Charity tomorrow. Understand?"

"Yes, Mom." She lunged at Charity, throwing her arms around her. "First thing in the morning."

"Bright-eyed and bushy-tailed," Charity said, trying not to grin. She was so damned cute.

After Flo trudged off to her cabin, Savannah pulled a bottle of white wine from the refrigerator and took two

wine glasses from a cabinet. "It's almost time for sunset. Let's go up to the bridge, shall we?"

"Sounds great."

The bridge had a teak deck that shone like new, a teak cafe table and chairs, and, in this anchorage, an amazing view to the west of Great Abaco Island.

Charity relaxed into a chair as Savannah yanked the cork from the bottle and poured two glasses. She handed one to Charity and sat down in the other chair.

Charity held up the glass. "To another fine day."

"To another fine day," Savannah said in agreement, clinked her glass, then took a long sip.

They sat there together for a full minute as the sun slowly made its way toward the horizon, a silence between them that started to feel uncomfortable.

Charity said, "Last time I saw you, you left without a goodbye." It was meant to be a question, not an accusation.

Savannah fidgeted in her chair. "Yeah, well. It was a little upsetting, you know."

"I know. I'm sorry."

Another minute passed. The sun barely moved.

"How's Flo handling it?" Charity asked, trying not to sound too intrusive.

Savannah shrugged. "Who knows. We talked about it. She thinks we got in a fight and ran away. I can't imagine what she'd be thinking if she knew the truth." She was talking, but not making eye contact.

"And she never will," Charity said. She meant it.

Savannah turned to face Charity. Her eyes had the same dull and inscrutable look as they'd had right after Charity had disposed of the bodies. "Why are you here?"

"Well, I..." *This was a mistake,* she thought.

Everyone she'd loved or cared about got killed, one way or another. She'd hoped she could leave those memories behind and have a normal life, if only for a few weeks. Spend time with a friend. Especially one who didn't look over her shoulder at every sound. Didn't she deserve that?

"I don't know," Charity replied. "I saw you were here and I... well, the truth is—" She drew in a breath. She could be honest with Savannah. That's what it meant to be a friend, right? "I know this will sound silly, but I don't have any female friends, really. You're as close to a friend as I've got, and I thought maybe..."

Savannah stared off into the sunset.

Maybe a friendship with Savannah was too much to expect. What happened on Hoffman's Cay was probably the most traumatic thing that she'd ever experienced and Charity's presence was bringing it all back.

"I know what happened must have really shaken you up," Charity said. "I hope my coming by to visit isn't too uncomfortable for you."

That still didn't crack the shell that Savannah had encased herself in.

Charity wasn't sure what to do, what else to say. She set her wine glass on the table and started to rise from her chair. "You know what? I should go."

Savannah seemed to snap out of her daze. "No, no. Please." She touched Charity on the arm. "Please stay. I've been rude. I'm sorry. Really."

Charity hesitated, then eased back into the chair.

Savannah forced a smile, let out a puff of air as if she'd been holding it in. "You were going to meet up with your boyfriend, after he had some boat repairs done, if I remember correctly? Are you still together?"

A wave of grief flowed over Charity. She gave herself a moment to let it pass. It had been nearly two years ago; she could say the words. "Victor's dead."

Savannah spun in her chair to face Charity. "My gosh. I'm so sorry."

"He was murdered in Nassau."

Her mouth dropped open.

Charity took a sip of her wine, then another.

Savannah wrapped her arms protectively around her chest. "Was he, uh, in the same line of work?"

"Yes, but he'd given it up. We both had. We were cruising, like I said. His murder was random. Wrong place at the wrong time. A gang of thieves drugged him and robbed him, then bludgeoned him to death."

Savannah shuddered. The tendons in her hand stretched taut and turned white as she gripped her wine glass.

"I'm sorry. I shouldn't have said that. Too much information, right?" This wasn't going as Charity had hoped.

A wry smile formed on Savannah's lips. "I guess I should be grateful that people like you are willing to do what you do to keep people like us safe."

Charity didn't know how to respond, so she said nothing. She stared into the glass of wine. She really could use a belt of whiskey right now.

"I'm sorry about Victor. I really am," Savannah said, almost in a whisper.

"Thank you."

The sun ducked behind the trees of Pelican Point on Great Abaco Island to the west and orange streaks shot across the sky, lighting the wisps of clouds from underneath, making them glow.

Charity drew in a breath. She'd try again. She liked Savannah and her friendship was something she wanted very much. She needed to lighten the mood. "How about you?" she asked, keeping her voice upbeat. "A boyfriend?"

"No." Savannah threw her head back and managed a dry chuckle. "No, no, no. Nope. Not interested."

"You'd mentioned an ex-husband, last time we spoke," Charity said, knowing full well that the ex-husband wasn't Flo's father. "He's out of the picture? He didn't want anything to do with Flo?"

Savannah's eyes flashed with disdain at the mention of him. "Are you kidding? Derrick doesn't know Flo exists. He wouldn't care about her if he did. Besides, there's a reason I divorced him."

Charity didn't ask. She was walking a fine line. Prying into stuff that was too personal wasn't going to help.

Savannah went on. "He could lose his temper, get violent, you know." She emptied her glass, set it down, refilled it nearly to the brim, and took another sip before continuing on. "If I questioned anything, I swear, it was like I'd challenged his very manhood. When I left him, it made him very angry. But don't misunderstand. He didn't miss me. It was just an affront to his ego that a mere woman would leave *him*."

"I've met a few guys like that," Charity said.

"Yeah, well, I was stupid enough to marry one." She shook her head, ashamed of the decision.

"You were young."

"The thing is, he wasn't like that when we were in school. He was fun, care-free. Then he went to work for his dad." A sadness came over her for a long moment, then she sat up straight in the chair. "Enough about him." She brushed the air with her hand as though sweeping him away. "So, have you been here in The Bahamas all this time?"

"Actually, since I saw you last, I sailed all the way to Australia and back."

Savannah's eyebrows shot up. "Really? That must have been quite an adventure."

"It was."

"What brought you back here?"

Charity hesitated. The last time she'd mentioned Jesse, Savannah had clammed up. The two had had a re-

lationship, but Savannah had left to give her ex another chance. "I had a passenger I dropped off in the Florida Keys." She paused. "It was Jesse."

"Jesse McDermitt?" Her eyes lit up, but she quickly tried to hide her interest.

"Yeah. He helped me sail *Wind Dancer* back from the west coast."

"Ah." She sipped her wine, then looked down into the glass, as if she wanted to crawl into it to hide. "How long did that take?"

"Three months."

"You went through the Panama Canal?"

"Yeah."

"Huh. I bet that was interesting."

Charity waited. Would she ask about him?

Savannah took another sip of wine, her eyes darting about now as she mindlessly rubbed her earlobe. "How is he? Jesse?"

"He's good. Real good."

Savannah turned to look Charity in the eye. "Are you and he...?"

"No." Charity shook her head. "No. Just good friends."

"Ah." She seemed relieved. "Well, a guy like that. He must have a girlfriend by now."

Charity shook her head. "Not really." He'd been seeing Sara Patrick for over a year. She was the first mate of *Ambrosia*, the ship Jesse was currently training on. She was Jesse's co-worker, and, as far as Charity could tell,

their relationship was purely physical, but then Jesse wasn't exactly the kind of man to kiss and tell.

"Not really? What does that mean?" Savannah said, staring at Charity.

Charity shrugged. "He's a man. How do I know?"

Savannah grinned and Charity laughed.

"Forgive me for saying it," Charity said, her tone soft, "but you seem like you still have feelings for him."

Savannah stared off at the sunset but said nothing.

Charity offered, "He's a good man."

Savannah jerked her head toward Charity. "I know that."

"I'm sorry, I didn't mean to..."

Savannah's eyes softened. "Sorry."

Carefully, Charity said, "You told me he might be Flo's father. Don't you want to know for sure?"

Savannah sat back in the chair, blew air out of her lungs in a long, exhausted exhalation. "Why? Does he want to be a father?" It was obviously a rhetorical question. "I'm so happy with just the two of us. Why bring a man into the picture to mess it all up?"

Charity held up her glass again. "I'll drink to that."

Savannah clinked her glass and gulped down the remainder of her wine. She set the glass on the table and crossed her arms in front of her chest. "The thing is, I don't know if I'd want him here, with her, anyway. What happened at Hoffman's Cay—it's made me think these last couple of years. Your life, his life, the things you do. It's not...I can't have that for Flo."

The acid in Charity's gut turned. The air around her closed in, murky and stale. Savannah was right. She was a killer. It wasn't just a job. She killed without remorse, without a second thought. With a gun, a knife, her bare hands—it didn't matter. She looked down at her own hands and she saw blood. Too much blood. She was coated in it. She couldn't touch Flo, couldn't be around her.

Suddenly Charity couldn't breathe. She pushed up from the chair. "I've gotta go," she managed to blurt out.

Savannah rose beside her. "I'm sorry. I didn't mean to—"

Charity didn't hear any more. She was down the ladder and into her dinghy, the motor started, and halfway across the water to her own boat before she breathed again. She tied off the dinghy and fled down below, to her bunk, where she flopped facedown in her pillow and wept.

She cried for all she'd lost. For a mother who'd abandoned her, a father who'd died in the prime of life, her childhood, her innocence. For Jesse's friend Jared, who Charity had fallen in love with, and for Victor. All lost too soon. For all that could have been but would never be, she wept.

She was who she was. She couldn't change that now.

She cried until she couldn't cry anymore.

CHAPTER THREE

Streaksof the morning sun shone in through the hatch, waking Charity. She lay on the bunk where she had collapsed the night before, still clothed. She hadn't moved all night. Dragging herself up and into the head, she stared at her reflection in the tiny mirror. A pathetic creature stared back at her. She couldn't remember the last time she'd cried or felt sorry for herself. It simply wasn't her nature.

What the hell is wrong with me?

She knew who she was. Savannah's declaration hadn't come as a surprise. In fact, she agreed that children should be protected, at all costs. And that included segregating Flo from the violence that had been a part of Charity's life for so long. It meant keeping Charity away. Wherever she went, trouble seemed to follow. She didn't want that for Flo. Or Savannah. They were better off without her.

So, why did she feel like the rug had been ripped out from under her?

Didn't matter. Dwelling on it wouldn't do any good. She would teach Flo to swim, give her a few tips she could practice, as she'd promised, then she'd make an excuse and move on. She'd leave them be; it was the right thing to do. She'd been selfish to want more from them.

After brushing her teeth and slipping into a one-piece swimsuit, she went through her usual routine to secure the boat, then fired up the dinghy and motored over to *Sea Biscuit*.

Savannah greeted her with a thermal carafe in one hand and an empty coffee cup in the other. "Black, right?"

"Right," she said, surprised she would remember. "Thanks."

"I'm glad you're here. Flo's been up for an hour. She wanted me to radio over, but I told her she had to wait."

Charity breathed a sigh of relief when Savannah didn't mention her hasty exit the night before. She secured the dinghy on the cleat, climbed the small ladder, and took one sip of the warm brew before Flo appeared. Bright-eyed and bushy-tailed was an accurate description. She was all pent-up energy, skittering about. "I'm ready. Are you ready? I'm ready."

"Let Charity have her coffee first," Savannah said in that calm tone Charity had heard so many times over the years from mothers other than her own. Hers had skipped out when she was a toddler, and she had no recollection of her. Had she talked like that? Was she calm and reassuring? Or was she a nervous mother,

worried about every little thing? Was that why she'd left? The reasons had always haunted Charity. Her father wouldn't talk about it except in whispered apologies when he'd been drinking.

For years, she'd tried to get information from neighbors and cousins, but no one would speak about her mother's departure. Either they didn't really know why, or they kept silent out of respect for her father. Charity always suspected it was the latter. After her father died, they were even more close-mouthed. The past was buried. Maybe it was for the best.

Though she couldn't help but wonder if the woman was dead or alive. If she ever found her, she'd ask her one question: why'd you leave? Charity was mature enough to understand that, whatever the reason, her mother didn't want to be there with her, and her childhood could never have been like Flo's, with a loving, patient mother. Yet, she would catch herself daydreaming about it. In her fantasies, her mother had long, blond hair that glowed in the afternoon sun. She always smiled, a warm, kind smile. And she smelled like fresh linen.

But those were the fantasies of a child.

Charity lifted her mug, gesturing toward the water. "Why don't you get in and show me what you can do?"

In a flash, Flo was down the ladder and poised on the swim platform, her hands above her head, ready to dive. "Here I go. Watch me." She leaped into the air, bent at her waist, and sliced through the water. When she broke the

surface, she wiped the water from her eyes and spun to see Charity's reaction. "Did you see? How'd I do?"

Charity gave her a thumbs up. "Now c'mon back." With her coffee in hand, she went down onto the swim platform.

Flo swam back and climbed out of the water.

"You really want to be a competitive swimmer?" Charity asked.

Flo's head bobbed up and down.

"It's a race, so it's all about speed. And to be fast, you have to be strong, with good technique, as well as efficient. Make sense?"

She nodded again.

Charity tapped the swim platform with her foot. "Don't think of this as a diving board, to jump from. Think of it as a solid brace to push off from."

"Okay." Flo's eyes were wide open as she hung on every word.

"That's what gives you speed. Then you have to keep it up."

Flo nodded some more.

"First, we'll focus on how to glide through the water with the least resistance. You need to have a sleek, streamlined body. So, raise your hands above your head."

Flo's hands shot up.

Charity grinned. She set her coffee cup down and raised her own arms in the air to demonstrate. "That means no arms flapping out to the side, no googly

elbows." She moved her elbows around loosely. "They're not chicken wings."

Flo giggled and started some kind of dance, squawking like a chicken.

"I said they're *not* chicken wings."

"Oh," she said, grinning, and straightened up.

"Do like I'm doing. Place one hand on top of the other and lock them together with your thumb, like this." Charity lowered her hands to show Flo how her left thumb wrapped around the outside of her right hand, then raised them again. "Now, you want your arms tight against your head. Squeeze tight against your ears."

Flo squeezed.

"Underwater, this whole part of your body doesn't move. It's like the front of a rocket, cutting through the water. Got it?"

Big nod. "Got it."

"Okay. Let's see you practice that part. As you enter the water, don't jump and dive. Instead, crouch down, then use your legs to push off the platform and enter the water like a rocket, your hands piercing the water to let you through."

Flo stared at her. "How do I kick?"

"Don't worry about kicking right now. Just practice that part, with your arms. Do it a couple of times."

She squeezed her arms tight against her ears, bent down, and launched. When she came up for air, Charity said, "Great. Now do it again."

Up the swim ladder she came, got herself into position, and launched again.

"Great. Now do it again," Charity repeated.

Flo dove once more. When she surfaced, she spun around. "How many times?"

"Oh, I don't know. Until you do it perfectly each time."

"How many is that?"

Charity raised her shoulders all the way up to her ears in an exaggerated shrug. "Dunno."

Flo didn't seem to like that answer, but she hauled herself out of the water and got into position to do it again.

Before she jumped, Charity said, "Do you know the difference between a professional and an amateur?"

Flo shook her head.

"An amateur practices until she gets it right."

Flo's eyebrows knit together slightly. She knew some bit of wisdom was coming.

"But a professional practices until she gets it right every time."

Flo's bottom lip pushed upwards. "Hm," she said. She might not have understood that now, but she would.

"Your brain knows how," Charity said, "but you have to do it over and over again for your body to remember, without you having to think about it. It's called muscle memory."

"Okay. I think my brain's ready to learn more," she said.

"I bet it is," Charity said, trying not to grin. "So, next I'm going to teach you the dolphin kick. Your arms stay up like I showed you, and your legs will stay glued together, too. Real tight. No gap between."

Flo slid her right foot up next to her left foot and squeezed her legs together. "Like this?"

"Good. Now, let's swim over into the shallow water where I can stand next to you."

"I'll race you," Flo said, her body arched and ready to go.

"You got it," Charity said and slipped into the water.

Flo dove and came up kicking.

Charity stayed one stroke behind her nearly all the way to shore, until the last stretch, when she powered past her.

They stood up on the sandy bottom.

"You've seen a dolphin swim, right?" Charity asked.

"Yep, like this," Flo said and made the motion with her hand.

"Exactly. Dolphins evolved from land animals with four legs, and over time, their hind legs disappeared, their tails became broad and flat, and their front legs became flippers. You're going to swim like a dolphin does, using its whole body." Charity patted her belly. "Think of your midsection as the center of all your power."

Flo patted her own belly, imitating Charity.

"Suck in your belly button and squeeze your butt cheeks."

Those little eyebrows shot up as she held back a giggle.

"I'm serious," Charity said. "You want a tight core."

Flo drew in a deep breath and held it.

"No, don't hold your breath. Just hold your muscles tight. Now, when you go under, move like this." Charity demonstrated the motion. "Like I said, like a dolphin. And when you kick, kick up and down, legs together. Push against the water both ways. One motion. Not too much one way or the other. No more than ninety degrees."

With a push off the bottom, Flo plunged into the water and moved as Charity had described.

"Good. You're doing great," Charity said, praising her when she popped up. "Keep it up."

Flo submerged again, moving through the water with her hands out in front of her.

"Excellent. Do you feel it in your feet?"

"I do. I really do."

"Good. Two more laps. Make small, rapid kicks."

Charity watched as Flo swam back and forth, kicking with all her might. She was one determined little girl. After several more laps, Charity told her to head to shore.

"I'm not tired," Flo said.

"I know. That's why we're taking a break. It's no good to get yourself exhausted. You need to practice a little every day, not all at once."

They waded to shore and sat down in the warm sand.

"Let's make sand angels," Flo said and lay down on her back.

"Are sand angels what I think they are?"

Flo moved her arms and legs up and down in the sand, pushing it aside and leaving a little winged-girl imprint. "C'mon, it's fun."

Why not? Charity thought. She lay back on the hot sand, spread her arms and legs out and swiped back and forth, swooshing the sand aside.

Flo giggled and Charity started to giggle too. It *was* fun.

"You're an angel," Flo said.

"No, you're the angel," Charity said, sitting up. She brushed sand from her arms.

"No, you are."

"No, you are."

"My mom said you're an angel."

Charity turned. "When did she say that?"

"When those bad men came, and you beat them up. She said you were a guardian angel."

"An angel, huh?" *More like a fallen angel.* So, she had remembered that much. "You know what, let's get back. I bet your mom has breakfast ready."

"I already ate breakfast."

"Well, lunch then."

They raced back to the boat, Flo giving it all she had. When they got there, she climbed out of the water onto the swim platform, then went right up the ladder to

the deck. Woden was waiting. He immediately circled his charge.

Savannah was waiting with a hairbrush in her hand. "Let's get that hair brushed before it dries in a tangled mess."

Flo backed away from her, reaching for the brush. "I can do it."

Savannah handed her the brush. "Okay, Miss Independent."

Charity didn't want to be presumptuous about lunch or anything else. She needed to make a graceful exit. "Now, if you practice every day, like I showed you, you'll be swimming like a pro in no time," she told Flo, staying on the swim platform.

"Oh, won't you stay for lunch?" Savannah said. "I've got all the fixings out for sandwiches. And homemade macaroni salad."

"Well, I should get going."

Flo poked her head through the rail. "Don't go. Please."

Savannah gave Charity a warm smile. "I'd really like it if you would stay."

Charity looked up at Flo's sweet face. "I am hungry after that swim."

"Yay," Flo said and rushed up the stairs to the bridge. Charity followed.

The food was all set out, lunch meat and bread on a tray, the macaroni salad in a resealable container.

"Help yourself," Savannah said from the deck below. "Would you like a beer?"

"Sure, thanks."

"I'll be right up with it."

Flo plopped down on one of the teak chairs and ripped open the bread bag. She took out two pieces of bread, dropped them on a plate, then another two and dropped them on another plate. "There you go," she said.

"Thanks. Will you pass the turkey?"

She handed over the package of sliced turkey breast. "I don't like turkey. I'm a ham girl."

"Oh, you're a ham, all right," Savannah said as she came up the stairs.

Flo stuck out her tongue.

"That's not very kind. Is it?" her mother said.

The tongue was quickly sucked back in.

Savannah handed Charity a bottle of Red Stripe as she said to Flo, "Tell me what you learned."

As Flo stacked her sandwich, a layer of ham slathered in mustard, then more ham slathered in more mustard, she babbled in her singsong voice about every detail of the dolphin kick.

"She's a good student," Charity said, when Flo's description finally petered out.

Before Flo took a bite, she spun the sandwich on the plate, tearing the crust off the bread, bit by bit.

Charity smiled. She'd done the same thing as a child.

Once the sandwich was to Flo's satisfaction, she crammed it into her mouth and bit off a mouthful. A dab of mustard stuck to her chin, but she didn't care. She didn't have a care in the world. Oh, how Charity envied

her. Somehow, just being with her helped Charity relax and live in the moment. She determined that she was going to do that, even if for only one more hour before she had to leave.

She'd never thought much before about why other people enjoyed children so much. To her, they'd seemed like a burden, a responsibility without much reward. Something parents endured. But Flo's enthusiasm—her uninhibited joy for life—was addictive. Charity wanted to feel that way every day.

"You've got mustard on your chin," she said.

Flo grinned, showing her big, awkward adult front teeth that didn't quite fit in her mouth yet. She flipped her sandwich sideways and used it to wipe the mustard from her face, then burst out laughing.

Charity laughed with her.

"For heaven sakes, don't encourage her," Savannah said, a hint of laughter in her own voice.

"You should listen to your mother," Charity said, trying to keep a straight face.

Flo giggled some more, that little girl giggle that was so infectious.

Charity washed down her own bite of sandwich with a swig of beer.

For three more hours, Charity stayed while Flo talked about her schoolwork, the dolphins they'd seen in the Turks and Caicos, and how she was going to build a robot someday. She even taught Charity about the constella-

tions, though it was daytime and they couldn't see them just then.

Charity couldn't remember a time she'd felt so relaxed, so content. But she'd promised herself she'd leave the next morning. It was selfish to want more time with Flo.

At about noon, she stood, stretched, and decided she really needed a swim. Three miles was her regular workout. She could swim the coast of Lynyard Cay south, which was about one and a half miles, then turn and head back.

"I'm going to go for a swim, get some exercise," she said.

Flo was on her feet. "Yeah, let's go."

Savannah shook her head. "Not so fast. I think Charity needs a little time alone."

Her eyelids fluttered with longing. "I'll be quiet, I swear."

"Flo, what'd I say?"

She kept her eyes on Charity. "Tomorrow then?"

Charity sighed. "I'm afraid I need to get going. I'll be leaving first thing in the morning."

"What? You just got here!" Flo didn't mask the whine in her voice.

Savannah looked at Charity, surprised. "I'm sorry to hear that."

"Well, I really should check in with my new employer," she said. She didn't really need to, but it was as good an excuse as any.

Savannah stared. Charity couldn't read her expression. Was she relieved? Disappointed?

Florence wrapped her arms around Charity's waist. "Please don't go."

Charity pulled away from her to gaze down at her face and smooth her hair back behind her little ears. "I tell you what. I'll go for my swim. Then, we'll grill hot dogs. Okay? We'll make it a big party. How does that sound?"

A party wasn't going to cheer her up.

"I'll bring the hot dogs." Charity tried to sound upbeat, but nothing was going to cheer her up either.

"That sounds great," Savannah said, a fake excitement in her voice.

Charity backed away from Flo and headed to her dinghy. She needed some space. Being here had stirred up so many unexpected emotions. She wasn't thinking clearly.

When she got back to *Wind Dancer*, she took a package of hot dogs from her freezer and set it in the sink to thaw. She checked her email. Nothing. Voicemail. Nothing. A swim was exactly what she needed. Swimming was meditation to Charity. She didn't think, didn't plan. She simply swam. The movements, the strokes, the repetition, pushing herself to her physical limits, all lulled her into a calm state of mind.

She slipped into the water. In no time, it seemed, she'd reached the southern tip of Lynyard Cay. She turned and swam back north. She was doing the right thing, she told herself. Savannah was right. Flo didn't need Charity in

her life. She would only bring her sorrow. They'd grill hot dogs, eat some ice cream, tell knock-knock jokes and before dawn, Charity would be gone. To Nunjack Cay, as she'd planned. To swim with the sharks and the rays.

Who was she kidding? She didn't give a shit about the sharks and the rays. She wanted to be with Flo. But she'd leave all the same.

Stroke, stroke. No thinking. Thinking led to feeling. She couldn't handle feeling right now. *Just swim.*

CHAPTER FOUR

Back at her boat, Charity checked for emails again. Nothing. Armstrong had no job for her yet. She was free to do anything. Whatever she wanted.

She scanned the chart. Sandy Cay, a world-class snorkeling spot, was nearby. The elkhorn coral there was amazing and the reef was known for spotted eagle rays and sharks. But she'd snorkeled there before. Hope Town was to the north a few miles. She could tour the famous Elbow Reef Lighthouse, one of the last working manual lighthouses in the world. The mechanics of the old structure had captivated Victor. Every two hours, the lightkeeper had to wind weights up to the top of the tower, where gravity would then take over, and, as the weights descended, the light would rotate every fifteen seconds. It was a fascinating feat of engineering. They'd planned to see it, but he'd been killed before they had a chance. Touring it now didn't sound all that interesting.

Unless maybe with Flo. It would probably be fun with her.

The hot dogs had thawed, but dinnertime was still a few hours away. She put the package in the refrigerator and grabbed a magazine from the shelf. After dropping Jesse off, she'd picked up the most recent issues of National Geographic and Cruising Outpost, her two favorite periodicals. She filled a bottle of water and headed to the cockpit, where she sat down, kicked up her feet, and opened the magazine.

On page seven, she looked up and realized she hadn't retained a word. She had no idea what she'd read, or even which magazine she held in her hands. Her mind was somewhere else. She closed the magazine and tossed it at her feet. She needed to get her head back together.

Over on *Sea Biscuit* there was no sign of anyone. What were they up to? Flo probably had some school assignment to do or needed to clean her room. Maybe she was helping her mom with laundry or something. Whatever it was, she was doing it with that zest for life that Charity wanted to find. She'd seen fleeting glimpses of it in Moana toward the end of their trip, and also in Fiona, though to a lesser degree.

Was there an age where it becomes irretrievable?

She got up and went back down below, taking the magazines with her. After placing them back on the shelf, she checked her email again. Still nothing. She glanced around the salon. The head needed scrubbing, so she got out her pail of cleaning supplies and went to work. The galley hadn't been cleaned in several days either, so when she finished with the head, she went to

work there, wiping out the refrigerator and the inside of the oven. Then she got out her mini-vac and vacuumed every corner.

She liked a clean boat. That was done. Now what?

She slouched down onto the seat. "What is wrong with you?" she said aloud.

The clock read 4:30. She could head back now. It wasn't too early. Besides, little girls ate dinner early so they could go to bed early, right? Maybe they could play a game before dinner.

She got up, packed the hot dogs in a cooler along with a couple of beers, grabbed a bag of potato chips, and headed toward *Sea Biscuit*.

Unlike the day before, Savannah seemed relaxed and comfortable with her arrival. She met Charity on the swim platform and grabbed the dinghy's painter, quickly hitching it on an aft cleat. Charity handed her the cooler and bag of chips. "I don't have any buns," Charity said. "I wasn't thinking."

"No problem. We'll use bread. We do it all the time. C'mon aboard."

Flo bounded across the deck, grinning. Her hair was pulled back into a ponytail and it swayed from side to side. "Wanna play Scrabble?" she asked. There was no greeting, as though their time apart had been a blink.

"Sure," Charity said. It wasn't a game she favored particularly, but she'd play anything Flo wanted.

"I don't like it, but my mom says it's good for me. Like broccoli."

"I see," Charity said, grinning at Savannah. "Broccoli is important."

She disappeared inside, then moments later reappeared with the board game under her arm. "On the bridge?"

"Sure."

Up the ladder she went. Charity followed. Flo spread the board out on the table and handed Charity the bag of letters as she sat down. "I'll keep score and you can check my math," she said.

"Sounds good."

A breeze blew through gently as Charity arranged her letters in the holder. "Feels like it might cool down tonight."

"You go first," Flo said.

Charity grinned at her. "All business. I see how you are."

Flo proved to be quite good at the game, but when Charity made the word "czar" on a triple word score, Flo frowned. "I don't even know that word. That's not fair."

"Well, now you do," Savannah said, joining them. "It's another title for a king or an emperor. It comes from Russia."

Flo crossed her arms and pushed her lower lip up into a pout. "Well, it can go back to Russia."

And Nadia Mikhailov, too, Charity thought. She'd taken the silver medal in Sydney, beating Charity by half a stroke, then soon after, defected to the United States, and became a media star. Her net worth was now

in the millions. Charity didn't care about the money. It was the Russian woman's reason for defection that irritated her. Political persecution. Charity knew, though, that she was just hungry for fame. The last time she'd read about Nadia, she was dating some rock star and driving the tabloids crazy.

"Why don't you go get cleaned up for dinner?" Savannah asked Flo.

Charity helped her put the game away and she slunk off to wash her face and hands, the box under her arm.

"She's such a doll," Charity said, as she disappeared down the stairs.

"Yeah, most of the time." Savannah shook her head. "But she has a stubborn streak."

"She get that from her mom?" As soon as Charity let the words loose, she regretted it. "I didn't mean—"

Savannah laughed. "Yes, she gets that from her mom. And two stubborn women on one boat can really be a problem sometimes."

While Flo was gone, Charity took advantage of the minute alone with Savannah to say, "I really appreciate you allowing me to come back for dinner, but I want you to know, I understand your concerns. And I don't blame you. I'll be gone in the morning."

"Oh, please don't go," Savannah said, her voice laced with regret. "I said things I didn't mean. Please forgive me."

"Well, I..." Charity was taken aback. "I'm not sure there's anything to forgive."

"Of course, there is. I opened my big mouth and said things I shouldn't have. Out of fear, I guess. It was stupid. You helped us that day. It wasn't your fault those men came along. And if you hadn't been there, well, I don't know what would have happened."

Charity nodded, not knowing what else to say.

"I owed you a big thank you, and instead I went and insulted you. I'm sorry. I just..." She sat down in the chair and sighed, as though releasing a heavy weight. "It's just when I saw you again, it brought back all those feelings. I admit, it scared me. It scared the hell out of me. And the thing is, it's so exhausting sometimes, keeping up with Flo, keeping her safe. And it's just me. Twenty-four-seven."

"I can't imagine," Charity said. Is that what being a parent was like? Worried every moment of every day? Always vigilant?

"Please don't rush off. Not on my account, anyway."

Charity nodded. She admired people who were honest and straightforward and Savannah was certainly that. "I appreciate that. Thank you."

"Besides, Flo is enjoying her time with you. It's good for her. And, if I'm honest, I could use some time with another grownup, too. Like you, I don't have that many girlfriends either."

Flo appeared, holding up her hands to show they were clean. "Can we grill the hot dogs now?"

"Sure can," Savannah said, pushing herself up from the chair. She descended to the aft cabin top, then headed

down to the small cockpit, where the tiny gas grill was mounted on the rail, hanging out over the water.

Charity followed, brought the cooler from the corner, and handed her the package of hot dogs.

Savannah said to Flo, "Will you find a loaf of bread and get the condiments out on a tray? We'll eat up on the bridge." Flo immediately obeyed.

"She really is a good kid," Charity said.

"Yeah," Savannah said with a proud smile. "She really is."

After the hot dogs were gobbled up and the potato chips gone, Charity convinced Flo to try another round of Scrabble. This time Savannah joined them. Soon, it was Flo's bedtime. Before Charity left, she promised another swimming lesson first thing tomorrow morning.

As Charity lay in her bunk that night, she felt at peace. She'd found her place, if only for a short time. She was happy. Perhaps happier than she'd ever been.

When morning came, she rose, dressed in her swimsuit, and headed right back to Sea Biscuit. She and Flo had work to do and there was fun to be had.

Soon, they had a regular morning routine. Diving from the swim platform, over and over. Charity always made sure to move on to something else before Flo could think the training too tedious. That was followed by

timed swims in the shallows, where Charity clapped and encouraged Flo to push herself. She quickly began to show progress.

On their fourth day together, after mixing a batch of no-bake cookies after dinner, Flo proclaimed they should have a sleepover on *Wind Dancer*. Charity's eyes immediately met Savannah's.

Savannah didn't seem concerned. "As long as it's all right with Charity," she said.

Charity nodded and Flo launched into another excited display, bouncing on the settee and hooting like a banshee. Woden jumped to his feet and paced about, looking for the source of the disruption. When he found none, he circled twice before curling back up into a ball and immediately going back to sleep.

"Get your things together," Savannah told her. "Toothbrush and PJs."

Flo raced to her room to pack.

"Are you sure you want to take her for the night?" Savannah asked Charity. "Do you know what you're getting yourself into?"

"Well, she can't possibly snore as loudly as Victor did. I was always worried when he exhaled, that the sails would come unfurled."

Savannah grinned. "No kidding? Jesse would—" Her expression changed in an instant. "Anyway."

Charity pressed on, as if nothing had been said, letting Savannah hide her comment. "With little girls, I assume it's all about the stories and jokes."

"And she hates to go to bed. It's always a fight now. Though with the swimming lessons and all the excitement of you being here, she's been passing out on her own."

"Mom!" Flo called.

Savannah excused herself to help Flo. As Charity washed the cookie pan and wiped up the galley, she pondered what to do with Flo on *Wind Dancer*. She didn't have any board games or TV, though she didn't see a television on *Sea Biscuit* either. She pretty much had nothing on board to do with a ten-year-old girl. Maybe she could go over some new swimming techniques or tell her stories about her competitions.

When Savannah returned, she handed Charity a clear-plastic storage box with a white lid. "In case you need something to do."

"Thanks. You read my mind," she said, relieved. In the box were some drawing pads, colored pencils and markers, some stickers, and two pairs of scissors. "Good thinking."

As they boarded the dinghy and headed over to *Wind Dancer*, Flo chattered away, ignoring her mother's prompts for good behavior and listening to Charity, especially about bedtime.

Charity glanced over her shoulder at Savannah. She stood on the swim platform, her arms crossed, her smile trying to hide her concern, but her eyes gave her away. Flo would only be a couple hundred feet away, but she would worry. That's what mothers did.

Except for my mother, Charity thought. She'd left when Charity was a toddler. Was it because she couldn't stand the worry? Isn't that what Savannah had said? The ever-present anxiety of caring for someone with unconditional love was exhausting. Maybe her mom just couldn't take the pressure.

Charity had had a taste of that pressure when those men had confronted them on Hoffman's Cay—the possibility of failure had been terrifying. But then, it had come after the fact. These last few days with Flo had made her truly understand what it meant to be vulnerable. Maybe because she'd been well-trained and possibly over-confident, she'd never thought about herself or her own safety. But to have someone else to protect, someone who couldn't protect herself? The responsibility was overwhelming.

Thankfully, the most important thing she'd have to handle was to make sure Flo brushed her teeth. For Charity, it was only for one night, but for Savannah, it was for a lifetime.

Flo, on the other hand, got to live in ignorant bliss. She didn't look back. As hard as that might have been for Savannah, Flo's independence was a good thing. It was a testament to Savannah's parenting. Charity's father had told her once: from the moment you have a child, your job is to help that child grow away from you. She could see now, exactly what he'd meant.

Once they boarded *Wind Dancer*, Flo waved at her mother, and Savannah finally turned and went inside. "What do you want to do first?" Flo asked.

Charity opened the companionway door and headed down below with the box of art supplies. "I was thinking we could draw or—"

"Draw what?" Flo was right behind her.

She set the box on the table. "Where's your bag?"

"Oh, yeah." Flo scurried back up the ladder, grabbed her bag, and started back down.

"Hold your horses." Charity held out her hands. "Hand that bag down so you have both hands for the ladder."

She did as she was told, then hurried down the ladder. "What do you want to draw?"

Charity's mind went back to her own childhood. Back to a time before her father had died. When everything was simple and nobody got hurt. She remembered a sleepover at a friend's, and how the girl's mom had helped them make paper dolls.

"Well, when I was your age, we made paper dolls. I thought that might be fun."

"What's a paper doll?"

Charity closed every door in her mind, save the memory of her friend's mom showing two little girls how to have fun on a rainy day. Mentally, she moved herself into that role, allowing it to fill her mind, and suppress all the tactical thinking that normally preoccupied her mental processes.

"What's a paper doll? Are you kidding? Paper dolls are so much fun." She took the lid off the box and chose a drawing pad. "I'll show you." She sat down at the dinette with Flo across from her. "First, you draw a doll. Make it fit the whole page. Like this." She started with the head, then added the body, arms, and legs, then drew on eyes, a nose, and a mouth. "If you want to give her different hairstyles, don't draw her hair on yet."

Flo watched as Charity drew her doll, then dug a pencil out of the box and sketched her own.

With the blunt-nosed scissors, Charity cut her doll from the page. Then she laid the cut-out on a blank page. "Then you trace the doll, ever so lightly." She used a pencil, showing Flo how to do it. "So you have the shape to draw the clothes. I'm going to make a dress for her first."

"Me too," Flo said.

As Charity drew a dress with a frilly skirt, Flo did the same. She used bright pink and purple to outline stripes. Flo diligently colored each stripe, making sure not to cross the lines. When she switched the pink pen for the purple, she started to hum. Charity didn't recognize the tune, but it was a happy, upbeat melody. It suited her perfectly. Flo was a happy, upbeat kid. She wasn't worried about her mom. She didn't wonder if the anchor would hold tonight or if the sky was falling. She lived in a state of joy, savoring each moment. Charity was determined to do the same.

"Now, when you cut out the dress, you have to leave tabs to fold over so it will hang on the doll, like this." Charity drew tabs on the shoulders and at the waist, then she cut the dress from the page, and folded the tabs so they would fit over the doll. "See?"

"That's cool," Flo said. "I'm going to make a bathing suit so my doll can go swimming."

"Great idea." Charity grinned. Her first thought was that a paper doll wouldn't last long in the water, but to Flo, it was all about the imagination. "I'm going to make a life jacket so my doll has one for sailing."

"Yeah," Flo said, tearing off another sheet of paper.

"What are you going to name your doll?"

"I'm naming her Charity."

"That's funny, I'm naming mine Flo." She chose a blue pencil and filled in the eyes. "See, it's you. Look at the blue eyes."

She smiled and her eyes sparkled. "I like making paper dolls."

"I'm glad," Charity said.

"My mom said I should smile and be courteous, even if I don't always get to do what I want to do."

"That sounds like good advice. We don't always get to do what we want."

"I know my mom gave you the drawing box. Is this what *you* wanted to do?" She looked at Charity with genuine concern.

"Absolutely. I can't think of anything else I'd rather be doing right now." It was the truth. "I knew we'd have

fun together, no matter what we did. But I admit, I didn't have a plan, so I was glad your mom suggested it."

"Why would you need a plan?"

"Well, I don't mean a plan, exactly. I just meant...well, actually, it's always good to have a plan. And it's especially important to have a plan B."

"What's a plan B?"

"I'm glad you asked. A plan B is a backup plan. It's what you've thought through to do if plan A, that's your first plan, doesn't go as you thought it would."

Her little eyebrows scrunched together. "I'm confused."

"You've helped your mom anchor the boat, right?"

She nodded.

"What would you do if the rode broke and you lost the anchor?"

She shrugged.

"Well, you have to do something. And you have to do it fast. You can't just let the boat drift into a reef, can you?"

"No."

"When you go to anchor, you have plan A. That's dropping the anchor, letting out the rode, then backing down on it to be sure it's set, and you're good, right? But what if something goes wrong? Then what? Plan B is what you've already thought to do if any of those bad things happen. So you're prepared and not freaking out wondering what to do when it does happen. Let's think it through. For example, what if the anchor gets stuck?"

Flo shrugged as she sorted through the colored pencils. Charity had lost her to the dolls. Oh well, Rome wasn't built in a day, and children didn't grow into adults overnight. She let it go.

By the time the clock turned to bedtime, they'd made a full wardrobe for their dolls—jeans, shorts, dresses, swimsuits, uniforms. Even hats.

When Charity told Flo it was time for bed, she got up from the table and went to brush her teeth and change into her pajamas without a word. No argument.

She's on her best behavior, Charity thought. *She wants to be allowed to come again.*

Charity tucked the paper dolls and supplies into the box and set it aside. Her own little Flo doll got tucked into her chart drawer. She folded the dinette down, got some blankets, and made a bed for Flo.

When Flo got into bed and pulled the sheet up, she looked up at Charity and smiled. "Always have another anchor ready."

Charity smiled back. "That's a good backup plan."

Minutes after she snuggled into bed, Flo was sound asleep. Charity leaned on the wooden mast, where it extended through the cabin top and down to the keel, gazing at Flo. It was like they say about sleeping babes; *all of God's grace in one tiny face.*

If Flo were her daughter, she'd never leave her side. How did Savannah do it? Charity's feet became rooted to the floor. She stood there, staring at this precious child,

until her legs went numb and she finally had to give in to her own need for sleep.

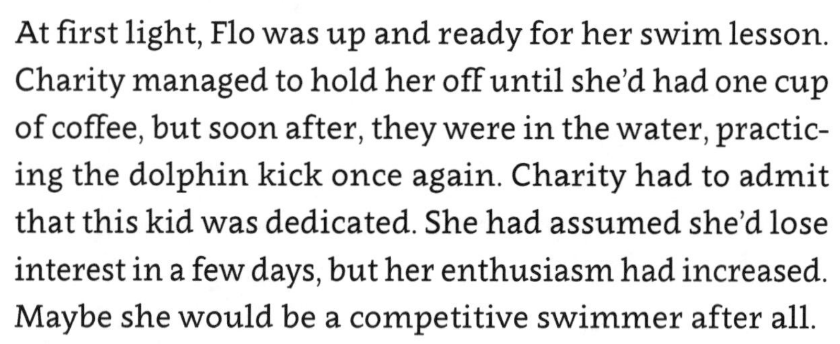

At first light, Flo was up and ready for her swim lesson. Charity managed to hold her off until she'd had one cup of coffee, but soon after, they were in the water, practicing the dolphin kick once again. Charity had to admit that this kid was dedicated. She had assumed she'd lose interest in a few days, but her enthusiasm had increased. Maybe she would be a competitive swimmer after all.

They ate lunch with Savannah, which included the no-bake cookies they'd made the night before. Then Savannah insisted that Flo get some schoolwork done. Charity excused herself, promising a picnic on the beach tomorrow to appease Flo, and went back to *Wind Dancer*. She set to work oiling the teak deck. It was long overdue and the work would keep her busy.

By late afternoon, she decided she needed a swim. Instead of her usual daily three-mile routine, for the past few days she'd only done short swims with Flo.

She changed into her swimsuit, locked the companionway door, and slipped into the water. It felt good to focus on her breathing as she moved through the water. Swimming truly was her meditation. By the time she reached the southern tip of Lynyard Cay, she was feeling like herself again.

A niggling voice in the back of her mind kept telling her that she should move on soon. Savannah had been gracious, asking her to stay, but there came a time when one, even when invited, would wear out their welcome.

She decided she'd enjoy two more days, then set sail to the north. She could always swing back by, or they could meet up somewhere else. There was no reason she couldn't see them more often. But for now, she should give them some space.

As she turned and swam back north, the whir of an outboard motor reverberated through the water. Charity popped her head up. A skiff zinged by with four men aboard, heading for the anchorage. Were those cops? What was that about? She dropped her head and kept swimming.

The engine quieted as the boat slowed. Charity looked up again. The skiff was pulling up to the stern of *Sea Biscuit*. What could they want? Four men. Woden's low, deep bark echoed across the water.

Something was definitely wrong.

Charity sped up.

The barking stopped. Did that mean Savannah knew the men?

She looked up again. She couldn't see if the men were still in the skiff. It was too far. Had they gone aboard? Inside?

She dropped her head again and kicked it up to a sprint. *Sea Biscuit* was still more than 500 meters away. She needed to close the distance. Fast.

A scream. Charity jerked up. A man walked down the side of the boat with Flo locked in his arms. She kicked and screamed. He shoved her down the ladder and into the skiff.

Adrenaline shot through Charity's veins. She had to get there. She had to stop them.

Then Flo let loose a scream that stopped Charity's heart.

She risked a glance as she pumped her legs and arms as fast as she could.

"Mom! Mom!" Flo screamed. Two men jumped into the skiff. The engine revved to life and they zoomed away. With Flo.

Her wails bounced off the wake left by the screaming outboard.

Charity was still 100 meters away. Fifty seconds. *Goddammit!*

Someone was in the water. Savannah. Facedown. But they had Flo. Charity could swim right to *Wind Dancer*, get in her dinghy and go after the skiff, but they'd outrun her with her puny ten-horse engine. And they had a head start. But maybe, just maybe, she could see where they'd go ashore. Though not likely. If she lost sight of Flo now, finding her again would be against impossible odds.

Or she could try to save Savannah, who might already be dead.

CHAPTER FIVE

The man had lunged at Flo, wrapped his gorilla arms around her, pinning her arms to her sides, and lifted her right up off the floor.

"Let her go!" her mom had yelled. Another policeman blocked her way.

"Mom!" She couldn't breathe. What was happening? "Mom!"

Her mother's eyes had flared with pure terror. Flo didn't understand. Policemen were supposed to help you. But these were not good guys. She knew by the way her mom yelled at them. She said they were liars. They were like the men Charity had beat up. They were mean.

"Charity! Help! Charity!" Flo kicked and squirmed. She had to get free. But the man clamped down tighter. "Let me go! Let. Me. Go! Woden!"

Her dog barked like crazy, but her mom had put him in her room and closed the door. He scratched at the door, woofing to be let out. He was supposed to protect her. Woden was a big, scary dog. Everyone was scared of him. But he was trapped behind the door. Why had her

mom closed him in? If he was out here, Woden would bite the man and he'd let go.

Flo kicked with her legs as hard as she could, but the man didn't budge. Out the door he went. The sun blazed in her eyes. "Mom! I'm scared. Mom!"

Where was her mom? Flo's heart was racing and her body started to shake. "Mom!"

He set her down on the deck and shoved her, trying to get her down the ladder. She grabbed hold of the handrail and wouldn't let go.

"Move it," he barked.

"Mom!" Where was she? *I have to hold on.*

The gorilla man clamped onto her wrist and yanked her hands from the rail. She screamed as loud as she could. "I don't wanna go!"

Another man grabbed her around her waist and pulled her into the skiff.

"My baby!" Mom screamed. She was at the rail. Then she spun and kicked at one of the policemen. He hit her across the face.

"Mom! Don't hit my mom!" He'd knocked her down. "No! No! Don't hurt my mom!" she cried and tried to stand but got yanked back down onto the hard seat. *Please, somebody help!*

One of the policemen jumped into the skiff, making it rock.

Then the other policeman was coming down the ladder. Her mom was right behind him. She kicked him in the head from behind. He swung around and grabbed

her leg, pulled, and she landed on her back with a loud crack.

Flo's stomach squeezed and she thought she was going to throw up.

The policeman went back up the ladder. Savannah got to her feet, but the man punched her in the face, and she tumbled over the rail and into the water with a splash.

"No!" Flo screamed. She lunged toward her mother, but both men grabbed her by the arms. Her head went dizzy and she couldn't breathe. "No!" Terror rose from deep in her throat. "Arrrhhhh!"

Suddenly, the engine roared in her ears and they were moving. Her mom was face down in the water.

"No! We can't leave her! She can't breathe. She can't breathe!" Tears blinded Flo's eyes. Snot filled her nose. "Mommy!"

"Shut up, kid," the man pinning her down said in her ear. "Shut up or I'll give you something to scream about."

She gulped for air.

"Your mom's a criminal. You're better off. Now shut up."

She squinted up at him through her tears. "Liar! You're a liar!"

His fat hand clamped over her mouth. It smelled of gasoline. Her eyes fixed on the long, dark hairs on his knuckles. Was he going to kill her too?

She froze, then looked up at the man steadily, holding her breath.

He removed his hand from her mouth. "Smart girl."

"That'a girl, Florence," the other man said.

Her head snapped back to face the man who'd spoken. "How do you know my name?"

"Your mom said it."

"No, she didn't." Flo clamped her teeth together and started to shake. These guys were definitely not policemen. These were bad guys. "You're a liar." She pushed up on her feet. She could jump out of the boat and swim away. But his hand was still there, holding her arm. She screamed as loud as she could.

"How about you shut up?"

Charity. Where was Charity? She'd save her mom. She was her guardian angel. Her mom had even said so. But where was she now?

"Chari—"

Flo was slammed backward and a rag was shoved over her nose and mouth. It smelled sweet. She struggled for just a moment.

Then she felt sleepy. So sleepy.

CHAPTER SIX

Charity swam straight to Savannah, her mind now in full tactical mode. Flo was long gone. There was no way she would be able to catch that boat. She might not be able to save Flo, but she had a chance of saving her mother. With her arm wrapped around Savannah's neck and shoulder, she dragged her to the boat and up onto the swim platform.

Savannah was unresponsive and not breathing. Charity pinched her nose, took hold of her chin, and tipped her head back. She delivered five rescue breaths, then began chest compressions. One, two, three. Five more breaths. She lowered her head and put her ear near Savannah's mouth, watching her chest for any movement. "Don't you die on me. Do you hear me? Don't you die."

Savannah started to convulse. First her head shook, then her body clenched at the waist, as her abs and diaphragm contracted to expel the seawater. Charity grabbed her by the shoulder and flipped her on her side as her body jolted back to life. A gagging sound rumbled

from deep in her chest and she retched hard, sputum and half the Caribbean flowing from her mouth, then immediately she began to hack and cough.

"You're all right," Charity said. "You're all right."

Charity held Savannah's head in her hands as she knelt over her, keeping her from rolling off the platform.

"Flo." She shook, her body trying to get air. "Flo."

"Just breathe. I'm here. Easy now. Breathe."

The rumbling in her throat morphed into a scream. Her hands grasped for something, anything, as she tried to get upright. She shoved Charity aside.

"Stay still and breathe," Charity told her.

Savannah gasped. "My baby!" Then she collapsed. But she was breathing.

The whir of the outboard motor was long gone. All Charity could hear was Woden, inside, barking wildly, his canine voice gone hoarse.

Savannah managed to push herself up again. Her head spun around as she scanned the water for the skiff. "Flo. We have to get Flo. They took Flo!"

"They're gone," Charity said.

Savanah swung to face her, eyes enflamed with anger. "What? No! We have to go. Now."

Charity shook her head. "I'm so sorry. They're gone."

"No! No!" She scrambled to her feet and fell again. "Oh God! No!" Her hand clamped onto Charity's elbow. "Why didn't you go after them?"

"I had to make a choice."

The woman shrank back, wracked with sobs. "You should have left me. You could have saved her."

"There was no way I could catch them. Their boat was faster. They already had a big head start." Charity hated having to say it, but it was the truth.

"No. No. No," Savannah cried, shaking her head. "We need to go now!"

Charity grabbed her by the shoulders. "Listen to me. It's going to be all right. Right now, I need you to breathe and think. Can you do that?"

Savannah collapsed in her arms, wailing. Charity held her tight, each sob ripping her guts out. But she couldn't go there. She needed to focus. Focus. For Flo.

"Can you stand now? With my help?"

Savannah gave no response.

Charity stood up and pulled Savannah to her feet. "You listen to me," she said firmly to her friend. "You listen to me right now. We're going to find Flo. But I need you to focus. I need you. Do you understand me? Flo needs you to focus."

The anger flared again in her eyes. "You should have left me."

"Good. You keep talking. Whatever it takes to fire those neurons. C'mon." She forced Savannah up the ladder. Poor Woden was still barking. "Let's let Woden out and you tell me exactly what happened."

Like a marionette without her strings, Savannah wobbled. Charity gripped her around the waist and walked her into the cabin. She set her down on the

settee, then moved to the aft cabin door and flung it open. Woden came charging out. The dog had all cylinders firing at once, sniffing around, barking and growling at nothing.

With an eye on Savannah, Charity flipped on the radar and AIS. There were no boats in the area. None moving away that might have Flo onboard, large or small. Nothing. The skiff had vanished.

As Charity turned back to Savannah, she noticed a drawer in the galley had been left open. And a cabinet door hung askew.

"You should have left me," Savannah cried again. "Gone after them. Then maybe..."

"But if I didn't make it, and you had died, I'd have nothing to go on." Charity found a towel and wrapped it around Savannah, then knelt on the floor in front of her and took her hands in her own. "Listen to me. You have information, whether you realize it right now or not. You're the key to finding her. I know this is hard. Look at me." Savannah's eyes slowly met Charity's. "Anything you remember will help. Do you understand? Whoever it was, they targeted you. Could have been last week, last month. That means you probably saw them, noticed something."

Kidnappings like this were almost never solved. Flo was gone. In the wind. And the odds were, they'd never see her again. The thought made Charity's throat constrict. They'd done it right in front of her and she'd been helpless to stop it. If only she hadn't gone for a swim.

She forced herself to take a deep breath. She couldn't go there. And she couldn't bear to give Savannah the devastating odds.

"Let's start with what happened today. Tell me everything you remember. From the beginning."

Savannah nodded, a subtle, barely noticeable nod, but she was coming around.

"Where's your phone?" Charity wanted to record her words, while they were fresh, in case she needed to go back later for any details that might have been missed or forgotten.

Savannah shook her head, an act of utter surrender. She didn't know where her phone was. Then her hand went to her shorts pocket. She held out the phone for Charity, but it appeared to have been ruined by the water. Charity tried to turn it on, but the screen was blank.

"Forget that," Charity said. "Tell me what happened." She quickly glanced at the radar. Still nothing moving.

Woden had exhausted his search around the boat and now nudged Savannah's knee. Her hand dropped to his head and she mindlessly stroked his ear. "We were working on some homework. On the deck. The skiff came. Right at us. Pulled up to the stern." She started to shake. "Oh my God, Charity."

"You're doing great," Charity said, trying to keep her own voice steady and calm.

Savannah gulped for air and continued. "There were four men. Two had Bahamian Police uniforms on." Her

expression changed, as though something suddenly made sense. "I knew they weren't police." She looked into Charity's eyes. "Why didn't I trust my gut?" The tears started flowing again and she shuddered with sobs.

"We're not going to second-guess everything. We're going to deal with the situation we have now. Just tell me what happened, exactly as it happened. Any detail you remember, tell me."

She sniffled. "They didn't look like cops."

"Why didn't they look like cops?"

"I don't know. They just didn't."

"Were they Bahamian?"

"Yes. The two cops. The fake cops. I think so. Then there were two white guys in street clothes."

"Did you notice anything about them or their clothes?"

Savannah searched her memory, then shook her head. "T-shirts. Jeans. One had a baseball cap on."

"The shirts or hat say anything on them? Logos? Anything?"

"No. They were plain."

"Okay, so they pulled up to the boat. What did they say?"

"They told me they had a warrant, that I should put Woden away and they were boarding my boat. I asked to see the warrant and the one stood and put a hand on his sidearm. I knew something wasn't right, but what could I do?"

Charity held her gaze, trying to keep her focused. "I would have done the same thing." It was a lie, but what good would it serve to tell her any differently? "Then what did you do?"

She started to hyperventilate. "I shut Woden in Flo's room."

"Slow down," Charity said. "Then the four men came aboard?"

"No. No." She shook her head, really concentrating now. "One stayed in the skiff."

"Which one?"

"One of the white guys." She huffed. "Oh God. Flo must be so scared. Oh God, Charity. Why? Why is this happening? Where'd they take my baby?"

"We're going to figure that out. We're going to figure that out together. Stay with me. Why is the drawer open?"

Savannah looked at the galley drawer in a daze. "They brought us inside, they opened them, went through stuff."

"You said they told you they had a warrant. Did they say what for?"

She nodded as though the memory had just come back. "They accused me of running drugs. They pulled a plastic bag of something out, a bag of drugs, like they'd found it in the drawer. Charity, I don't—"

"I know. I know you don't. Then what happened?"

Her eyes squeezed shut. "They took Flo. They took my baby."

"So, they pulled out a bag and showed it to you, said it was drugs? Did they say anything else?"

She wiped snot from her nose with the back of her hand as she shook her head.

Charity got a roll of paper towels from the galley, ripped off two sheets, and handed them to Savannah.

"They took her in the skiff." She blew her nose in the paper towel. "I tried to stop them. I kicked one in the head. Then, I..." Her eyes darted about as she tried to drag the memory out. "I don't remember, it was two big men. One hit me and I went over. I must've blacked out."

"Have you ever seen any of these men before?"

"No. Not that I remember. Except..." Her eyes stopped moving.

There it is, Charity thought, seeing the flicker of recognition in her friend's eyes.

"What?" she asked.

Savannah rubbed her head. "I don't know."

Then she was sobbing again, and Charity held her in her arms, shaking inside. Who would do this? What kind of men would rip a child from her mother's arms?

She knew these kinds of men. She'd faced them before. And if it took the rest of her life, she was going to track them down like the evil scum that they were. If she had to cross every desert, comb through every cockroach-infested city, she'd get Flo back. Then she was going to rip their black hearts from their chests and impale them on spikes.

CHAPTER SEVEN

"Did I ever tell you that you screw like a tiger, baby?" Derrick slapped his mistress on the ass. "Like a tigress in heat." He grunted as he pressed against her. She was bending over in front of him. He liked it like that, taking her from behind.

"Mmmhmm. Every time, baby." She moaned in a way that made her sound like a purring cat.

"Well, you do. Like one of those circus tigers. Maybe I should get a whip. Huh? What would you think of that? A whip?" He reached down and pulled the belt from his pants. "I think you deserve a whipping since you've been such a naughty girl." He folded the belt in half and pulled it tight, snapping the leather together. "Beg me not to."

"Don't do it."

"Oh, I'm gonna do it. I'm going to whip you until your skin is red and raw. Fifty lashes. Would you like that? Fifty shades of red? I want to see your blood, baby. I want to lick it."

"Mmmhmm."

"Beg me not to do it. Tell me you haven't been naughty." He snapped the leather belt again and the sound made her clench. "Oh, that's so hot. You've been naughty, haven't you? Maybe I should tie your hands to the bed post. What do you think of that? You need to be punished."

"Shut up already. You run your mouth too much."

She meant it. He hated when she ruined the mood like that. He tossed the belt aside. "That's what I love about you," Derrick said. "You don't take any shit. God, you're so hot." He ran his hand down her back, admiring her milk chocolate-colored skin. *If my father only knew*, he thought. He'd have a damned heart attack and flop right over on his desk like a fish out of water. Derrick smiled, imagining his father's face turning red, then white as he flopped around, trying to suck in air, but getting none until he collapsed, froth oozing from his mouth. *Sayonara, asshole.*

"Hey, what's wrong?" Chandra had pulled away, was staring at him.

"Nothing." He shook his head.

She nodded toward his waist.

He looked down. Limp. Again.

"I got shit on my mind, okay? Give me a break." He collapsed onto his side, rolled over, slapped his feet on the tile floor, and headed for the bathroom. "It's this goddamned heat." What was it about The Bahamas? It was supposed to be some kind of beach-lovers' paradise. But it always stank like rotting garbage and overflow-

ing sewage. "Doesn't anyone believe in air-conditioning around here?"

He plopped down on the toilet. "Where's the goddamned toilet paper?" he shouted through the bathroom door. *I swear to God, that woman does it on purpose.* "Don't I pay you enough money so you can buy goddamned toilet paper!"

The door flung open and a white roll of Charmin came at him like a missile. The door slammed shut.

"Thank you!" *Bitch.*

Derrick straddled the porcelain pot for ten minutes before getting back up. He wiped his ass four times. *How do people live without toilet paper?* he wondered. *That's just wrong.*

Before he headed for the bed, he popped a pink tablet of X into his mouth, one of the new bunny pills that was all the rage, washing it down with a glass of water. That would do the trick. Calm his nerves and get him going again. This was a new cut from the new supplier, more potent than the old shit.

Chandra was still in bed, lying on her belly, sprawled across the white sheets in her red lacy whatever-you-call-it, her eyes closed.

Derrick stood there a moment, admiring his woman. She was what they called *full-figured.* A whole lot of woman to handle. That's how he liked it. He'd had enough of skinny white bitches whining and carrying on. They always wanted something from him. Money, drugs, prestige. But not Chandra. She was her own

woman. She didn't take shit from anyone. He loved her mouth most. She said things that would make his dad blush, that was for sure. And gave the best blowjobs on the planet.

He was getting hard again.

"Wake up, woman." He pounced on the bed. "Don't think I'm doing all the work here."

Chandra came alive, flipped him over onto his back, and crawled on top of him. "Shut up," she said and slapped him across the face.

He moaned. "Oh, yeah. You know how I like it, baby."

His phone rang. "Oh, crap." He groaned.

"Don't answer it," she said, and slapped him hard again.

"Get off me. You know I have to answer it." He shoved her aside and skooched off the bed. "Where the hell is it?" He picked his pants up from the floor and shoved his hand in the pockets, one at a time, until he found the phone. "Yeah?" he said after punching the *Talk* button.

"We got the girl. Delivery on schedule."

Something didn't sound right. "Why do I hear a *but*?"

"But, uh, you didn't say the mom could fight. She attacked us, man. One of the guys had to fight back. She went down."

"What do you mean, *went down*?" A little snake started writhing in Derrick's gut.

"She's dead, man."

Oh shit, oh shit! No, no, no. He went into the bathroom and slammed the door. In a harsh whisper, he

said, "What'd I tell you? Plant the drugs, get out. What the hell happened?"

"Does it really matter?"

He was going to wring the man's neck with his bare hands. "Of course, it matters, you dimwit! Jesus Christ, I send you to do one thing. One thing, Donny."

"Well, it wasn't me."

"*Does it really matter?*" He said it in a snide, condescending tone, mimicking the dumb bastard. "What the hell do I do now?" He paced across the tiny bathroom and back. "Are you sure she's dead?"

"She was floating face down in the water when we left."

"Shit!"

"I thought you wouldn't really care since she—"

"Oh, shut up, Donny." He disconnected, flung the bathroom door open, and threw the phone across the room. It hit a framed picture of a rose on the wall, shattering the glass, and knocking it to the floor, where it broke into three pieces.

"Hey!" Chandra jumped up. "My momma gave me that."

"Oh, fuck." He slumped onto the side of the bed and held his head in his hands. "Why do I get stuck with these losers? Send 'em to do a simple job and they fuck it up, every time."

She sat down next to him. "What's wrong, baby? What's happened?"

"Nothing." Suddenly he could feel the X kicking in.

"It ain't nothing. You broke my momma's picture."

He sat up straight and pulled her toward him. "Screw your dead, fat-ass momma's picture."

"Hey!" She shoved him back. Man, she was strong for a woman. "Don't talk about my momma like that."

"What?" He grinned and grabbed her breasts, one in each hand. "You know I like my women built for comfort. More cushion for the pushin'."

"Yeah, how would I know? I'm still waiting for some. You been all up in the bathroom and on the phone. You better bury that white face of yours between my legs and make it up to me."

"If you purr like a tiger for me."

She fell back on the bed, grabbed his hair on either side of his head. and pulled him down onto her, arching her back. "Rrrrr."

He pawed at the red lace.

Then he remembered the girl. "Dammit! I can't. I gotta go." He grabbed his pants and flew out the door.

CHAPTER EIGHT

Charity got up from the seat and paced to the radar screen. "We need to call the police. We need to report Flo kidnapped right away so they can monitor the airports, the ferries." As she said it, she knew that if these men were pros, it wouldn't matter. They knew what they were doing. They wouldn't try to take Flo through an area that might be canvassed.

Savannah sat upright, suddenly alert. "What if they were police? Corrupt police? Then what?"

"You said they never actually showed you a warrant, right? And the way he brandished the gun—" She shook her head. "They weren't police."

Something bothered her about the story. Something didn't fit. Why would they come dressed as police? And only two of the four? She wanted Savannah to go through it again, but she wasn't sure her friend could take it. "You said they accused you of running drugs? And they had a baggie? Are you sure there were drugs in the baggie?"

"Well, no. They just said so."

"But that's when they accused you and then took Flo, right?"

"Yes. But, Charity, I don't run drugs. Of course, I don't. It's weird though..."

Charity stepped forward. "What?"

"Last week, when we got back here from Turks and Caicos, when I called customs for entry, they came out and searched *Sea Biscuit*, from bow to stern. I'd never had that happen. They took over three hours to do it."

"They say anything?"

"No. And I didn't think to ask. At the time, I figured it was a random check."

Had they suspected some drug activity then? But the men who'd come now weren't real cops. Were they? "But just now, these men, they actually held out a bag of drugs, in front of you and Flo, as proof?"

"Yes. I mean, I assume that's what it was. That's what they said. It was a green baggie with yellow tape. It looked like pink pills inside but—" She shrugged, unsure. "I don't know. Could have been M&M's for all I know."

"Why would they do that? Who were they trying to convince? You know they weren't your drugs. Were they trying to convince Flo?" Then it hit her. "Oh shit! Did you see them leave anything?"

Charity rushed to the galley and pulled out drawers, shuffling through the contents quickly. Her hand landed on a stuffed plastic baggie. She pulled it out. It was green with yellow tape and stuffed full of bright pink pills.

Ecstasy. *Shit!* She spun around. "Savannah, listen to me. Did they go into any of the berths?"

"No."

"Okay. Do exactly as I say. Check every corner, every crevice of every part of the boat they went in. If they stayed here in the main cabin, then only search here. Do it right now. Where's your spare anchor?"

Savannah stared, unmoving, her eyes wide. "My what?"

"Your spare anchor. You must have one. Where is it? Up front or in the stern?"

"The stern locker, but—"

"Do what I said. Now." She knew it came out harshly, but she didn't have time. She needed Savannah moving and moving fast. "Check every corner, every compartment of every part of the boat they went in for any more bags. Got it?"

Savannah nodded.

"And hurry!" She pushed through the door and headed for the stern. The anchor was where Savannah had said. She hauled it out of the locker and untied the rode.

Savannah called out. "I've found two more bags."

Charity scanned the horizon but saw nothing yet. She headed back inside to check the radar. There was movement beyond Pelican Point to the north-northwest. "Incoming vessel. Five miles out." She snatched the bags of drugs from Savannah's hands. "Are you sure you checked everywhere?"

Savannah shrugged, her mouth hanging open. She was terrified.

"Okay. You're doing great. Get your passport and swim to *Wind Dancer*. Swim straight there now. I'll be right behind you. Take Woden."

"But what are you—?"

"Just do it."

Savannah nodded. She ducked into her cabin and was right back out with two passports in her hand. "I've got Flo's, too."

"Good thinking." Charity grabbed a roll of duct tape she'd seen in one of the drawers.

As Savannah dragged Woden into the water, Charity taped the bags of drugs to the anchor, wrapping the tape around several times, then heaved it overboard and dove in after it. On the sandy bottom, she dragged the anchor into the shadow cast by the boat where it couldn't be easily seen in the crystal-clear water. She pushed it under the sand, then, using her hands, mounded sand on top of it, covering it as best she could.

Using the boat to push off, she headed for *Wind Dancer*, dolphin kicking nearly all the way, and caught Savannah as she got to her stern. The two shoved the soaking wet Woden up into the cockpit and crawled after him.

Charity unlocked and opened the companionway. "Now go down below and stay down there. Keep Woden quiet."

Savannah did as she was told without questioning.

The distinctive buzz of an outboard engine came from the north. A real Bahamas Defence Force patrol boat came around the bend at Pelican Point with two very serious-looking police officers aboard.

The sun had fallen behind the island and it was nearly dusk. Charity sat down in the cockpit and put her feet up, trying to look relaxed, like she was watching the sun set, like any other day.

The patrol boat went right to *Sea Biscuit*. The engine was cut and they tied off to the stern. The two police officers called out to anyone aboard. When they got no answer, they boarded the trawler, leaving the Defence Force officer with his boat. They carefully trod across the deck; weapons held in front of them.

Once they were inside and the driver was looking away, Charity ducked down below to check on Savannah.

"Make sure you keep Woden—"

The big dog lay sprawled on the floor, a hunk of Charity's leftover dinner under his paws. He lifted his head and growled, a low, menacing warning.

"I found half a T-bone in the fridge," Savannah said.

"Good thinking," Charity said as she slowly backed up the ladder.

After what seemed like an hour, one officer got back in their boat and the driver puttered toward *Wind Dancer*.

As his bow gently touched *Wind Dancer's* stern, the policeman reached out to grab hold. "Hullo, miss," he said. Definitely Bahamian.

Charity was on her feet. "Good evening."

He gestured toward *Sea Biscuit.* "D'yuh 'appen ta know where di owner of dat boat might be?"

Charity shook her head. "No, sir."

"Have yuh seen anyone comin' or goin'?"

"No, sir," Charity said again. "The boat was anchored there when I pulled in yesterday. I haven't really noticed anyone around."

"Di dinghy is still dere, but no one is aboard. Don't yuh find dat odd?"

Charity shrugged. "Now that you mention it, I guess. Maybe he left on another boat?"

She purposely said *he*. Most boaters were men. She wouldn't give away that she knew the owner was a woman. A little disinformation went a long way—a tactic Jesse had taught her.

The other officer stepped out from the cabin on *Sea Biscuit* and yelled across the way. "I've found something." In a gloved hand, he held up another green bag.

Oh fuck, Charity thought.

CHAPTER NINE

The police left after midnight.

Savannah stared with zombie-eyes through the porthole at the white wake they left on the surface of the sea.

Woden had finished the steak and was sprawled out on the floor, covering every inch of it, sound asleep, his stomach making gurgling noises.

Charity stepped over him to get to her phone. This situation was getting more complicated. She needed help.

Savannah came alive then, springing to her feet. "I need to go back to my boat. I need to—" Her eyes darted about, glazed with exhaustion. "I need to..."

"Savannah, you can't go back to the boat. If they catch you there..." She shook her head. "They found drugs on board. Do you understand that? That makes you a person of suspicion. They'll be back soon to impound the boat and if they find you there, they'll arrest you."

Savannah stared through Charity, seeing nothing, her mouth open and lips quivering. She looked as if she

might collapse. Charity gently guided her to sit back down.

"I need to get you to a hospital. The time in the water, you could have—"

"No!" That brought her alive again. "No. We find Flo. We have to find Flo."

"Okay. We're going to do just that. I'm going to start by calling for some help."

She opened the chart drawer where she kept her satellite phone and found her paper doll with Flo's blue eyes lying on top of a chart looking up at her. The air left Charity's lungs. She gripped the drawer handle and puffed, trying to get a breath.

"What's wrong?" Savannah said.

"Nothing." She grabbed the phone and slammed the drawer shut.

"Are you sure you're all right?"

"Yes, I just, I just thought of something."

"What?"

"I'm not sure if it's important." She had nothing. "Let me just make a call." She dialed Jesse's number, keeping her eyes on Savannah. It went straight to voicemail. "Call me as soon as you get this." She probably sounded like a crazy, desperate woman, but she didn't care. She was.

Next, she tried Chyrel Koshinski, Jesse's computer genius. She was the best hacker on the planet. She could get information on anyone and that's what Charity needed right now.

She answered on the first ring. "Hi, Charity. What's up?"

"Hi, Chyrel. I need your help, but I need to talk to Jesse first. He's not answering. Do you know where he is?"

"Yeah, a job came up and he's deep under. It's only a few days, maybe a week. Can it wait?"

"No. Highly critical."

"Well, how can I help?"

"Can you hack into the Bahamian police database?"

"Are you serious? What's happened?"

"I'm in the Abacos with Savannah Richmond. Her daughter, Florence, has been kidnapped."

"Holy crap! You mean Florence, Jesse's—"

"Yes."

"Good lord! How could anyone know she's his? Or do you think it's random?"

"I don't know. What I do know is it's complicated. At approximately 5:45 p.m. four thugs, two dressed as cops, planted drugs on Savannah's boat and took Flo. When Savannah fought back, they left her for dead. The real cops conveniently arrived right after the incident."

"And Savannah is—?"

"Alive. I was close. Not close enough to stop the kidnapping, but I was able to resuscitate her."

Savannah whimpered. Charity took hold of her hand and squeezed.

"You want to know what the cops know," Chyrel said.

"Exactly."

"Hold on the line. Give me just one minute."

Charity could hear the chatter of Chyrel's fingers on her keyboard, the click-click of her mouse.

"I'm in. Piece of cake. Now to find"—click-click—"here it is. An anonymous tip was called in about suspected drug activity on Savannah's boat, *Sea Biscuit*. Officers were dispatched. Looks like it was the second anonymous call. The records indicate that customs officers did a search on entry and found nothing."

"Affirmative," Charity said.

"That's all I see."

"Well, they'll soon be back to the office with evidence. Can you get me that report when it's filed?"

"Sure, but I don't know what we'll learn from it to find Flo. Maybe if they connect those drugs to a known dealer, I guess, but that's a long shot. Meanwhile, what's your plan?"

"Not sure yet."

"Well, whatever you need, call me. Any time of the day or night."

"Thanks," she said and disconnected.

Technology was an amazing tool when it worked. Charity thought of the camera she had mounted on the mast of *Wind Dancer*. If only she'd had it turned on and recording, Chyrel could run it through face recognition and maybe one of those thugs would pop up. It would be something. Right now, they were in the dark. Two anonymous calls. Dead end.

If this was about kidnapping Flo, why'd they make the call to get the boat searched a couple weeks ago? And if

it was about framing Savannah for drug-running, why take Flo? Why send fake cops? And why show her the bag of drugs, making a big show of accusing her? And in front of Flo? That point bothered Charity the most. It made no sense. If anything, if they were smart, they would have stashed the drugs to be found by the police without Savannah knowing. It was as if they wanted her to react. Or they wanted it to look legit, somehow. But for whom? Flo? A ten-year-old girl? That didn't make sense.

Maybe this was all about Jesse. Did they think he'd be watching? Were they expecting him to come running? If someone wanted to hit Jesse where it hurt most, killing Savannah and taking Flo was the way to do it. A ballsy move, but it would do the job. As far as Charity knew, she, Jesse, and Chyrel were the only people who knew that Flo was Jesse's daughter. Savannah professed that she didn't know, but Charity thought that maybe she did. Not by way of any DNA test or anything, but sort of a sixth sense or something. Maybe when Jesse called her back, she shouldn't tell him. He'd never forgive her, though.

Damned if I do, damned if I don't. If she got some possible suspects, she could run them by Jesse, see if he recognized anyone, without revealing the details. That could work. If she could get a damned lead.

Savannah slumped forward, let her elbows land on the table and held her head in her hands. "Why did I let them board? Why did they do this to me? Why did they take her!" Tears dripped onto the tabletop.

Charity steeled herself. She couldn't let Savannah sink into oblivion. They had to focus. "Dwelling on what we should have done doesn't get us anywhere. We deal with what we face, right here, right now. I want you to sit up straight and think. That's how we get Flo back."

Somehow Savannah gathered the strength and did as Charity demanded.

"Now think back. We're going to go over it again. Step by step. Then you're going to tell me about Turks and Caicos. Every moment of every day, until we find something."

Savanna nodded, swallowed hard and wiped her eyes with the backs of her hands. "We were...we were working on homework." The flood gates opened again, and she slumped back onto the table, face down.

"All right, let's just..." Charity needed some air. She wanted to flop down next to Savannah and cry her eyes out too. But she couldn't. She had to act. There was a clue. Somewhere. There had to be. Deep in the recesses of Savannah's brain, she knew *something*.

Charity went to the head, found a full roll of toilet paper, brought it back to Savannah, then sat down beside her. "Cry if you need to but talk. Over the last month, did you have any strange encounters? Any feelings of being watched? Anyone seem out of place?"

Savannah shook her head, a helpless look on her face.

"How long have you been back in country from Turks and Caicos?"

"About two weeks."

"And did you stop anywhere?" Charity sat back. "Why did you come this far north so fast?"

"I told you, I'm planning to meet some other families in Hope Town with kids Flo's age." Her eyes closed and she drew in a long breath.

"Okay. Did you stop anywhere?"

She nodded, but kept her eyes closed. "Eleuthera. Just overnight. Got provisions and fuel."

"And nothing happened there? Nothing that made you feel uncomfortable?"

"No, nothing."

"You haven't noticed a boat following?"

"No, but I wasn't looking, I guess." Savannah blew her nose in a handful of toilet paper.

"Okay, let's go back to today. Start at the beginning." Charity prompted her. "Flo was doing homework. Then four men arrived in the skiff."

"Yes." Savannah nodded. "Two were in police uniforms. But I don't think they were real police."

"Why?"

"Real police don't kidnap little girls." She had to blow her nose again.

"Okay, but before that. When did you suspect they weren't real police?"

"The way the one showed his gun. He said he had a warrant. But he didn't hand me a paper, he showed me he had a gun."

"It was a threat."

She nodded.

"Keep going. You need to tell it. Then what happened? Step by step, every detail you remember."

"Then three of them boarded *Sea Biscuit*. One stayed in the boat." She hesitated.

Charity felt a sliver of hope. There was something there. "Tell me about the one who stayed in the boat."

"I don't know. He...he stayed in the boat."

"He was white?"

"Yes."

"He was the driver?"

"I don't think so."

"Why would he be the one to stay in the boat, then?"

"I don't know. But I don't think he was driving when they approached." She dropped her head and pulled at her hair. "I'm not sure."

"All right. It probably doesn't matter who was driving. But when I asked you about him earlier, you hesitated. Like maybe you had seen him before?"

She lifted her head and her gaze turned inward. She was thinking about it.

Charity got to her feet. The possibility that Savannah had something, a clue, some kind of lead, was palpable. She didn't want to influence it. She kept her voice calm. "Just close your eyes. Picture him. Take your time. What was it about him?"

With a tiny glimmer of hope in her eyes, she nodded in agreement and closed her eyes.

"Try to focus on his face."

"I know it wasn't recently," she said, barely a whisper. "It's almost like..."

"Like what? Say it. Whatever comes to your mind. Say it out loud. You never know what it might lead to."

"Like I knew him, from somewhere, like—omigod!" Her eyes flew open as she jerked upright. "I think it was Donny." She shook her head. "No way. It couldn't be Donny."

A flutter of excitement stirred in Charity. She had something. "Who's Donny?"

"I'm not sure it was him."

"Who's Donny!"

Savannah's lower lip quivered. "A friend of my ex-husband. From high school. But—" She shook her head again, dismissing the thought. "I haven't seen him since, I don't know when. Years."

"What's Donny's last name?"

"Okay, okay. It's um... Mac. McSomething." She shook her head with frustration.

Taking her on a different tack might jar the memories. "What was the name of the high school?" Charity already had her phone back in her hand, ready to dial.

"McLaughlin. Donny McLaughlin." Her eyes fixed on Charity. "I don't know if it was him. But that's who I was thinking of. The guy looked like Donny McLaughlin."

Charity punched redial. Chyrel answered right away. "Go."

"I need a South Carolina DMV photo for a Donald McLaughlin. Can you—"

"Say no more. Give me a moment. And... sending it to your phone."

An image of a bearded, ratty-haired man in need of a shower popped up on her screen. She flipped the call to speaker and held the phone for Savannah to see. "Chyrel, you're on speaker now." Charity wanted her to be aware Savannah was listening, to be gentle.

"Roger that."

Savannah's hands jumped around on the table. With her right index finger, she jabbed at the phone. "That's him. That's the man who was in the skiff." For the first time since Charity had pulled her out of the water, Savannah looked like she might survive. Hope was an amazing thing.

Chyrel added. "I've found him listed on flights to Marsh Harbor, two days ago. Already on the second leg headed back to Savannah/Hilton Head International. That's your guy."

Savannah looked dazed. "But why would...?"

"Bingo," Charity said, realizing who the kidnapper was. "I think your ex-husband found out about Flo."

Savannah came off the seat like a jaguar let out of a cage. "That son-of-a-bitch!"

CHAPTER TEN

The ride in the skiff wasn't very long. Or was it? Flo had gotten sleepy after the gorilla man had covered her nose and mouth with that rag. But she was awake now, the situation coming back to her in bits. Her nerves made her shake. She didn't want to cry, but she couldn't help it. What were they going to do with her?

The driver pulled the skiff up to a dock and she was yanked by the arm up and out of the skiff, then led to shore.

"Where are we going?" she cried.

"Keep walking," the gorilla growled.

She could barely see through her tear-filled eyes. "I can't. I can't."

He lifted her, like he'd done on the boat, and carried her up some stairs toward a house.

She was groggy and tried to kick free, but he had her pinned in his arms. "Where are you taking me?"

He didn't respond, simply set her down at the top of the stairs on the edge of a big white porch.

She froze in place, her body shaking with fear. She wasn't sure she could stand on her own.

A sliding glass door rolled open and two people came out of the house, a man and a woman she didn't know. The man gave gorilla man a nod and he left her standing there alone. She wanted to run, but they were on a steep hillside, with bushes all around. There was nowhere to go but down the steps after the gorilla man.

The woman rushed toward her. She was tall and skinny, too skinny, and all smiley. She wrapped her arms around Flo. "Oh my, you must be so terrified, you poor thing."

Flo pulled away from this stranger. She didn't want her touching her. She smelled like fake, flowery perfume. It got in her nose and she didn't like it. She didn't like this woman at all. "I want my mom."

"C'mon, let's get inside," the man said, his eyes darting around as if he were afraid that he'd be caught doing something he shouldn't be.

"I don't want to go inside," Flo managed. She didn't want to go anywhere. She knew better than to go with strangers. "I don't know you. I want my mom. I wanna go home."

The skinny woman bent down so her face was at the same level as Flo's. "I'm so sorry, Florence. I know this must be very scary for you. If you'll just—"

"How do you know my name?" The gorilla man had known her name, too. She crossed her arms over her chest, hugging herself. "I don't know you and I'm not

going anywhere with you. I don't care if you know my name. I don't know you."

"Everything will be all right. We're not going to hurt you, honey." The woman shifted back upright and smiled, showing perfect, pearly-white teeth like those on the models in magazines trying to sell clothes and makeup.

She wasn't fooling Flo. "Don't call me honey! Don't call me anything." She backed away.

The man grabbed her by the elbow. "We're going inside. Now." He forced her to move forward, across the big, white porch, by the fancy white deck furniture, through the sliding glass door, and into the living room. He guided her to a big, fluffy, orange couch and when she didn't want to sit, he gave her a look of warning that was unmistakable.

She plopped down in the seat and the tears welled up. "I want my mom."

"I bet you do," he said, all snotty. "You're just like her. Stubborn as a mule."

Why was he being mean? This was like being in a scary movie and he was the bad guy. The tears came again. She didn't know what to do.

"There, there," the woman said. "Everything's going to be all right. I'm your mom now."

What? Flo's eyes grew large. Was she kidding? "You are *not* my mom." She covered her eyes with her hands. "I wanna go home."

"This is your home now. With us."

"No! You're lying. You're not my mom and this is not my home." She shot up from the chair, but the man was right there. He shoved her back down.

"Calm down."

She curled into a ball, as small as she could, and sobbed. "I want my mom."

He got right in her face, his stinky breath puffing at her when he said, "Your mom was the liar. She's a criminal. She broke the law. And criminals don't get to keep their children."

"She did not!" Why was he saying these things?

"She did," he snarled.

"Derrick," the woman said. "It's not her fault. Give her some space. This must be very traumatic." She stepped beside him and dropped to a crouch in front of Flo. "Everything will be all right. I promise."

How would it be all right? Her mom was floating in the water. She might be dead. Unless Charity had saved her?

"You'll see," the woman said, taking her hand.

She yanked it back.

The woman frowned. She stood back up. "Come with me. I have something for you. A wonderful surprise."

"I don't want your surprise," Flo said, spitting as much venom as she could. "And I'm not going anywhere with you. I'm not stupid. You're trying to trick me. You think I'm going to fall for that?"

"Honey, I'm not trying to trick you. We're not going anywhere. You're already here. I just want you to see your new room."

Flo's lip quivered. This was crazy. Nothing was right.

"Figures. Ungrateful. Just like her mom," the man grumbled.

The woman held out her hand and smiled. "I promise. I'm not going to hurt you. I think you're really going to like it."

If she went with this woman, would it get her away from the horrible man? Flo rose from the couch but refused to take the woman's hand. She followed her up a flight of stairs, down a short hallway, and into a bedroom.

The big bed in the center of the room had a pink bedspread covered with dolls and stuffed animals. It looked like a toy store she'd been in back in Beaufort with her grandmother. It was fun looking around in Monkey's Uncle, but Flo would trade all those toys for Charity's paper doll. Charity. What would Charity do now?

"Isn't this nice?" the woman said with a hopeful smile.

"I hate dolls." She didn't, but she wasn't going to let this woman think she could make her happy.

The woman's smile turned to a pouty frown. "I got you some new clothes, too. Would you like to see?" She went to the closet and pulled out a pink frilly dress.

"I hate dresses."

"Well, honey, I don't know what you want."

"I want my mom. And my dog."

"We'll get you another dog."

"I don't want another dog! I want Woden!" She tilted her head back and screamed. Why wasn't somebody helping her? She wasn't supposed to be here.

"Calm down," the woman said, taking her by the shoulders and shaking her.

She screamed louder. Someone had to hear her.

The man appeared at the door. "Shut up right this instant or I'll give you reason to scream."

Flo clamped her mouth shut, but she couldn't stop crying.

"You scream like that again and I'll show you what a belt across your behind feels like."

Flo shuddered, trying to stifle her tears.

The woman tried to smooth her hair. "You need some rest."

Flo jerked away from her. She crawled up on the bed, amid all the brand-new stuffed toys, buried her head under the pillow, and cried and cried.

CHAPTER ELEVEN

Anna pleaded with her eyes. "You can't go back to Beaufort right now. She just got here."

Derrick turned away from her. He knew what was coming. Her voice would turn into that shrill whine that sent irritating shivers up his spine, like when someone dragged their fingernails across a chalkboard.

"So?" he said. "What do you want me to do? I have business to take care of. What did you think was going to happen?"

"I didn't think you'd abandon us so soon."

"Jesus, Anna. You got what you wanted. Can't you be happy?"

Her face fell, and that lower lip curled into a pout. He hated when she did that.

"Please, Derrick. She's a scared little girl. She needs this time to bond with us."

Bond? Where did she come up with this shit? "She'll be fine. I gotta get to work."

Nag, nag, nag. That's all this woman did. *I want a baby.* Now she had one, maybe she'd shut up.

She followed him into the bedroom. "How long are you going to be gone?"

"I don't know. A couple weeks." He could feel her tense up. He needed a new tactic. He moved in, put his hands on her hips, pulled her to him, and ran his nose along her neck up to her ear. He knew she liked that. "You know what a slave driver my dad is."

She nodded in surrender. Thank God. He thought he was going to have to endure another round.

He escaped into the bathroom and popped another blue tablet into his mouth, one of the kind Chandra called kickers, just to calm his nerves. When he emerged, he stuffed his shaving kit into his carry-on bag and headed for the door. Anna scurried after him for a kiss, like a poodle in heat.

He gave her a peck and slipped out the door.

His taxi boat was waiting at the dock—a basic three-seater, center-console model with a 150-horse Tohatsu on the back. Plain white. Derrick shook his head. The man had no style.

Randall had become his regular driver here in The Bahamas, on the water, and on the big island. "Randall, my man," he said as he boarded.

Randall politely nodded, then shoved off from the dock once Derrick was seated.

"Boy, you've got the life, man. I bet you've got a woman on every island, eh?"

Randall grinned, but said nothing. He turned the wheel and pushed down on the throttle. The little boat

roared to life and they were quickly up on plane and zipping across the water.

"Ah, a man who doesn't kiss and tell," Derrick said, raising his voice to be heard over the hum of the outboard motor. "I respect that, man. I do."

The ride wasn't far. Derrick checked his phone. No messages. What the hell? His peeps were supposed to check in. He had a big shipment on its way to the States. He'd have to ride their asses again. Why was it so hard to get competent help?

As they slowed to enter the Abaco Beach Resort Marina, he said to Randall, "Hey, I've been meaning to ask you. Any chance you can help me score some X?"

Randall stared, scrutinizing him. "What yuh want dat for?"

He gave him an innocent shrug. "I just wondered if you could get me some."

What Derrick really wanted to know was if Randall might be a dealer for him. The man ran a lot of tourists in and out of the resorts. They had to be looking to score while they were here. Too dangerous to bring on a plane.

"Maybe." He paused. "Fuh yuh?" A little shrug. "I dunno."

"You get a lot of call for it?"

"What dat mean?"

"Do others, you know, Americans that you drive, do they ask for it? Or other stuff, other drugs?"

The man shrugged. "Dey kin ask."

Derrick frowned. He wasn't getting anywhere with this numbnut.

Once they were at the dock, he hopped out of the boat and checked his watch. Too bad the flight took off in less than two hours. He didn't have time to stop by Chandra's for another romp. He pictured how she'd looked earlier, bent over in front of him, wearing that red lacy thing. Maybe there was a later flight. He clicked through his phone and found the airline schedule. He was booked on the last flight of the day. *Damn.*

The phone buzzed in his hand. It was Anna. He hesitated before clicking to accept the call. "What?"

"Are you sure you can't stay at least one more day? I mean, this poor girl—"

"We've been over this. Jesus, woman." He hung up. He couldn't take the nagging. What was it with women? Always wanting something, begging him for it. Pathetic creatures. His mom had been the same way, but his father let it roll off. *Like water off a duck's back, son,* he'd say. *Women are delicate, needy things. Good for one thing, and one thing only. Don't let 'em drag you down.*

No need to worry about that, Pop. You haven't met Chandra.

Chandra. His mind went back to her bedroom and then an anger welled up in his gut. His loser henchmen had ruined a good afternoon with her. He'd felt the X kicking in right when Donny called. Losers had no sense of timing.

At least he was excited about the new pink bunnies. They were already selling like hotcakes.

Maybe he could swing taking the first flight in the morning. He started to click through his phone but thought better of it. His dad would have his ass if he was late to work tomorrow.

He followed Randall to his black, four-door plain sedan. *Geez, could this guy be any more boring?* Derrick thought as he got in.

After the quick ride to the new airport, Derrick breezed through security, and four hours later, after two mostly uneventful flights, he arrived in Beaufort—the land of antebellum mansions, pecan pie, and frilly white girls made of porcelain. God, he hated it there. The second leg of the flight was marred only by the one uppity stewardess running out of whiskey and scolding him for having to take a piss during the final approach to Savannah.

As he pulled into the driveway and hit the button to open the garage door, he said aloud, "Now, there's a classy place. I bet a rich guy lives there. Oh, right. Yep. Rich and successful... not to mention damned good-looking."

After he downed a double of Wild Turkey, his usual nightcap, he hit the sack. Alone. The way he liked it. Ah, the peace and quiet, with no nagging woman in the house.

At five in the morning, Derrick rolled out of bed, showered, and headed for the office. He swallowed a kicker with his coffee. He was going to need it to spend the day with his father. Good old Daddy-O. On second thought, he took another one.

He barely had a foot in the door when his father bellowed from his office, "Get in here, son."

Derrick gripped his travel coffee mug like the handrail on a rollercoaster ride.

"Sit down," his father said. An order.

Derrick bent at the knees and landed in the chair.

"Where have you been?" With that perpetual scowl on his face, his father stood next to his high-backed leather chair behind his shiny mahogany desk.

Derrick didn't make eye contact. That was always asking for trouble. "I told you. I had some personal stuff to take care of."

"Did you now." It wasn't a question. His nostrils flared. They always flared like that when he was angry. Even when Derrick was a little boy, he knew to watch for the nostrils. Now, he expected it, watched, amused by how his old man's nose hair twitched even though it made him quiver, knowing the axe was going to fall.

His father, Harold P. Coleman-the-fricking-III, crossed his arms in front of his chest. "Do I have to remind you? That's my name on the door. Do you think, after all I've done to build this firm, that I'm going to let you—"

Derrick rose from the chair. He had to get in front of this. "Tear it all down? No, Dad. We've had this conversation before. I just needed a couple days off to take Anna somewhere."

"Well, next time you *need a couple days*, don't let it happen right in the middle of a capital case. I need your brain here, son. I need you focused."

"I am focused."

"Are you?"

"Yes." His teeth locked together into well-worn grooves.

"Because if you're not—"

"Dad!"

"Good." He slapped the top edge of the chair. "Now let's get to work." His eyes fixed on Derrick's with steely determination. "Because I'll be damned if I'm going to lose a case to some smart-mouthed, colored lawyer."

Derrick's head swiveled to make sure the door was shut. "Dad, you need to be careful about that stuff. He's African-American."

"Oh, don't you start with me. This is my office. I know the difference. I'm not out on the damned street, glad-handing." He glared at Derrick, then his gaze settled on him with a look of disappointment. "I swear that woman must've been whoring around. You can't possibly be my son."

That stung. Derrick said nothing. He'd learned over the years when to keep his head down and his mouth shut.

"Where is Annabelle anyway?"

"She needed a vacation."

"A vacation? By herself? What the hell for?"

"Dad, everyone needs a break now and then."

"What does she need a break from? She's got one job." He grinned. "Giving me a grandson."

"Don't start with that."

"I don't know what the hell's the problem. Isn't she fertile? Maybe you should take her to see that doctor I told you about."

"Dad!"

"Well, don't blame me. Are you sure it's not you?" He leaned across the desk, narrowed his eyes. "Are you having trouble in that department?"

Derrick clamped his mouth shut, shaking. *Why do I put up with this?*

"Whatever. Just figure it out. It's getting embarrassing. And I'll never understand why you picked this one, anyway. At least Savannah had the hips for it." The finger came up, pointing at him. "You made a big mistake not breaking that filly."

Derrick cracked his knuckles, first his right hand, then his left. *Wait'll you find out what your precious Savannah has been hiding all these years.*

"Can I go back to my office now? I've got work to do."

The senior Coleman threw up his hands. "No one's keeping you."

CHAPTER TWELVE

Charity had to sit down; she was so relieved. The air left her lungs in one big whoosh. She didn't realize how long she'd been holding it in. "This is good. This is good news," she said. This she could deal with. She had somewhere to look, someone to target. There would be a trail. "Really good news."

"What?" Savannah stared. "My baby is kidnapped by my crazy ex-husband and you're relieved?"

"Charity's right," Chyrel said, still on the line. "If Flo had been targeted by traffickers, you'd never—"

"You know," Charity interrupted. "Let's not go there." Savannah didn't need to hear all the terrible possibilities.

"Right. Sorry."

"What Chyrel means," Charity said to Savannah, "is that, with your ex, he probably—" She almost said, *won't kill her*. But she really didn't know what was going on yet and she didn't need to put that image in Savannah's head. Better to stick to clear, concise facts. And anything that would keep Savannah calm. "He's probably taking

care of her. Because, I assume, this is about you. Right? He's making some kind of statement?"

"God knows what he's thinking and God knows what he'll do." She paced, throwing her hands up. "He's not the man I used to know. The people he's gotten messed up with. And now he's got my girl."

"Okay, let's take a breath. What do you mean, the people he's messed up with? What's going on?"

"This is revenge for me leaving him. That's what it is." She wasn't answering. She was on a rant now, jabbing her finger at the air. Charity decided to let her go, let her get it out, and, in the meantime, see what she might glean. Then she'd sift through it. "He's stealing her just to spite me." Savannah's eyes glowed with rage. She was getting more worked up. "And that son-of-a-bitch got a two-fer. He's framing me for drug running. Omigod." She slumped down, collapsing onto the settee as the full weight of it dawned on her.

"I knew this would happen. I knew some day he'd get revenge. He's heartless. I swear, he's an empty husk. He couldn't stand that I left him. It wasn't that he cared about me. It was the humiliation. The blow to his ego. And, wow, that man can hold a grudge. I just never dreamed...then...that he could..."

She finally lifted her face to make eye contact with Charity. What Charity saw in those eyes tore at her heart. "He's got my baby." She was spiraling downward fast.

"Not for long," Charity said.

Her words didn't move the woman. Savannah's gaze dropped to her hands and she stared, lost in a hopeless slump. "I'll be in prison. He really thought this through. God, he's evil."

"I'm not going to let that happen."

"Trust me. Derrick's got money, power, connections. And he hates me. It's going to happen."

Charity couldn't stand seeing her hurting like this. "Well, Derrick hasn't met me yet."

"But what can you do now? It's done. The police have found drugs on my boat. You said it yourself, I'm a fugitive." Her eyes flitted around. "No doubt he's thought of everything. He's probably been planning this for months." She huffed. "He's holding all the cards."

Charity reached out and grabbed her hand and squeezed. "No, he isn't. We are. You know why? Because you know him. Look at me." Savannah slowly raised her head again. "You know how he thinks. You know his fears, his weaknesses. That gives us the upper hand. Trust me. He's already played his hand. We are the ones holding all the cards now."

She didn't seem convinced. But she didn't know what Charity was capable of.

"Most importantly," Charity went on, "he has no idea we're on to him. In fact, right now, he probably thinks you're dead."

"Being dead can be a huge advantage," Chyrel said.

Both women turned toward the phone, and Charity smiled. "Yes, you're absolutely right, Chyrel."

Savannah got a look on her face as though she thought they'd both lost their minds.

"What she means," Charity said, "is if Derrick thinks you're dead, he won't know you're a threat. He'll relax. He'll let his guard down. If he was expecting you to get convicted of running drugs, then he expected a long custody hearing. He must have been prepared for that."

"Yeah, I bet he was. He's an attorney."

Charity nodded. "Makes even more sense knowing that. He would know to keep Flo hidden away until you're convicted. But if he thinks you're dead, he might bring Flo out of hiding right away because there'll be no one to argue for custody."

"My mom would. She's still alive."

"Doesn't matter. If he's the father."

Savannah's eyes met Charity's. Did she see a hint of a smile there? Charity knew Derrick had no legal claim to Flo. But did Savannah? Jesse had ordered a DNA test and confirmed Flo was his child, but he hadn't told Savannah. Not to Charity's knowledge. But the fact remained, Flo was not Derrick's daughter. And now he'd kidnapped her.

Charity grinned with the knowledge that when they straightened this out, he'd be in a world of shit. "We have an ace up our sleeve."

Savannah sat up a little straighter but said nothing.

Charity let that go. If Savannah didn't want to talk about it right now, she wasn't going to force it. She plowed onward. "You mentioned other people that he's

gotten messed up with. What exactly did you mean by that?"

Savannah tried to pull herself together. "Since we divorced, I've heard rumors that he's gotten into selling drugs. He runs ecstasy or something, sells it to high school kids. Well, he doesn't, but people who work under him do." She shook her head. "He's such an idiot."

Charity nodded. "The drug connection. At least it all makes sense, him using the drugs to frame you."

Savannah winced. "Yeah, I'm screwed."

"Not necessarily. Yes, right now, we have to assume you're a person of suspicion in The Bahamas. We'll deal with that as soon as we can, but Flo is our first priority. I want to confirm he took her and find out where he's keeping her."

Chyrel piped up. "I can fix that."

Charity had forgotten she was still on the phone. "What?"

"Her status as a person of suspicion. I can fix that right now."

"How?"

"Simple. A report of *Sea Biscuit* being stolen from the customs dock thirty minutes after it was inspected and judged to be clean. Just give me an hour or so to create it, back date it, and put it in their files."

"You're a genius," Charity said. Why hadn't she thought of that?

Savannah stared at the phone. "You can do that? Just like that?"

"Well, I'll need about an hour."

"Okay, but I don't understand how that would even work."

Charity answered. "Boats are stolen and end up getting used for drug running all the time. The reports are real easy to forget. Chyrel will find an officer who had a lot of activity that day and put his name on the report."

"Then we should report the kidnapping, too," Savannah said.

"Not a good idea," Chyrel said, sounding more sympathetic. "A kidnapping? Here in the States, the FBI would be involved. There...? Do you want the Bahamian police investigating it? You'll have to decide how you want to handle that one for real. Maybe staying dead is the best choice, I don't know. But I do know this, Savannah, you can trust Charity. Listen to her. She's a professional. She knows what she's doing. I'd rather have her looking for me than all the Bahamian cops put together."

"Thanks for all your help Chyrel," Charity said. "I know it's late. We'll check back first thing in the morning." She disconnected the call and turned her focus to Savannah. "I know it will be difficult, but you need to get some sleep."

"Sleep? With my baby out there? Are you kidding?"

"I'm not kidding. You need to try."

"But I can't. I can't lie down and just do nothing."

"You won't be doing nothing, you'll be sleeping, which is vital for you to be able to think. And I need you to be

able to think," Charity told her. "Do you understand? You're no good to her if you're exhausted. She needs your brain on full power."

Savannah stared. A hint in her eyes revealed she knew Charity was right. Even if Savannah wanted to, Charity doubted she'd be able to sleep. She knew the feeling. She didn't know if she'd be able to either, but she had to. For the same reason.

"Do you trust me?"

It wasn't a fair question. Frankly, she hardly knew Charity. But circumstances had brought them together, and no matter what it took, she would find Flo and get her back.

Savannah managed to nod.

Charity got some Benadryl tablets from her first aid bag and handed two to Savannah. "Take the forward berth."

After she made sure Savannah took the pills and was at least lying down, she went back to the chart drawer, pulled it open, and gazed down at the blue eyes of the paper doll. "I'm going to get you back. You hang in there. I'm coming to get you. Do you hear me? I'm coming."

Charity gently closed the drawer and released the breath she'd been holding. She needed to take her own advice and get some sleep.

She pulled a blanket from under the dinette, turned off the lights, and curled up on the bench seat, tugging the blanket up over her.

Moonlight lit the cabin with an eerie glow. Everything was scarier in the dark of night. Her thoughts went to Flo and the fear that precious little girl must be feeling right now. Her fists clenched. *That man had better not hurt one hair on her body.* Tomorrow. Tomorrow she'd find him. She released her fists and was fast asleep.

Before dawn, Savannah was up, which got Woden up. The dog paced, which was not an easy task for a 120-pound dog in the cramped quarters of her sailboat.

"He needs to go to shore," Savannah said.

"Okay, we'll take him in the dinghy."

Charity grabbed a couple of cups of yogurt from the refrigerator and two spoons.

Getting Woden into the tiny boat proved to be a challenging task, but they managed. Charity pocketed her cell phone and they headed for shore.

She handed Savannah the yogurt. "You need to eat."

While Savannah paced, eating the yogurt and waiting for Woden to find the right spot to lift his leg, Charity called Henry Patterson. Henry was one of Jesse's most trusted friends. He'd once served with Jesse's grandfather, fighting the Japanese in the Pacific, and the bond the two men shared had extended to Jesse. Henry would help, without question. He owned a little marina and mini resort on the north end of Andros Island, about 100 miles southwest of their anchorage, and Charity kept her helicopter at the San Andros Airport.

She quickly explained the situation, leaving nothing out. She trusted him. He agreed to let Savannah and

Woden stay with him and would send a go-fast boat right away to pick them up. He knew a guy, said he could be trusted, and assured her the boat would arrive within two hours.

"Have the boat driver pick us up in Little Harbor," she told him. "I need to secure *Wind Dancer* on a mooring."

"Will do," he said.

"Oh, and, I'm not sure we should mention this to Jesse yet."

"Understood," he said and hung up.

She then made the call to the fixed base operation at the San Andros Airport requesting that her bird be prepped and ready for a late morning departure.

Once Woden had done his business and they got back aboard *Wind Dancer*, Charity pulled anchor and set a course for Little Harbor, three miles to the south.

She called Chyrel to confirm the stolen vessel report had been filed.

"Done," Cheryl said. "Now I'm working on a full report for you on Donny McLaughlin and Savannah's ex, Derrick Coleman. Anything in particular I should look for?"

"Everything and anything you can find. Your usual magic. Donny first. I'm going to Beaufort to find him."

"I'm on it."

"Thanks. As soon as I'm—"

Savannah said, "*We're* going to Beaufort."

Charity kept the phone to her ear but shifted it from her mouth and shook her head. "That's not a good idea."

The look on Savannah's face was pure determination. "I heard you talking to that Henry guy. While my daughter is out there, God knows where, there's no way in hell I'm going to sit on the beach, drinking rum, waiting for someone else to find her."

Apparently, she'd rushed through the shock and denial stage and was in the full-on anger stage. "It's too risky. You have to lay low. There's probably a warrant out for your arrest."

"There's not," Chyrel said. "There was, but I made it disappear."

Charity was relieved but concerned. Having Savannah along was a recipe for trouble. To Chyrel, Charity said, "I'll call you back once I'm in the air."

"I'm serious," Savannah said, her body tense. "You said yourself, I'm the one with the information, the insight. I know Derrick. I'm going with you."

Charity gave her a slight nod, but she wasn't comfortable with it at all. For one thing, she would have to temper her normal way of handling things. "The thing is, this could get rough. I might need to—"

"Handle this like you did those slime balls on Hoffman's Cay? I understand. Whatever it takes. I want my daughter back. I don't care how you do it...how we do it."

Charity could see there was no point in arguing. "You're still going to have to stay in the shadows. If you're seen, Derrick could spook."

"I can do that."

"Listen, the thing is—" She stopped, drew in a breath, tried again. "If you go with me, I need you to trust me. Your emotions are all over the place. I need you to put some faith in my judgment and when I ask you to do something, I need you to do it. Do you understand?"

Savannah nodded, and she meant it, but from Charity's experience, when emotions were high, all bets were off. Her gut told her to leave Savannah on Andros with Henry, where she'd be safe, and Charity could do her job the way she needed to. But how could she tell her to sit by and wait? She had no idea what torture this was for Savannah. No, she'd take her, and do her best to keep her safe. And busy.

She hoped she wouldn't regret it.

"Okay, I need you to do something right now." She handed her the phone. "Call the police. Check on the status of your stolen boat. Make a big fuss, demanding information."

"What if they don't tell me anything?"

"Doesn't matter. I want another record on file of you reporting the boat stolen with a real interaction with a real officer. And to see how they react to you." She trusted Chyrel's abilities completely, but she wanted a memorable interaction recorded.

Savannah nodded in understanding.

While Savannah was on the call, Charity gestured for her to take the helm and slipped down below. She tossed some clothes into a backpack with her toiletries,

her laptop, and her Colt 1911. She filled a second bag with clothes she thought might fit Savannah.

Charity got back topside as they entered the narrow channel into Little Harbor. She took the helm, found an available mooring, and quickly got *Wind Dancer* secured. In the dinghy, she ran to shore to pay the fee and, not five minutes after she was back on board, a bright red and yellow-striped Cigarette boat pulled into the harbor.

"That's our ride," she said.

Savannah finally hung up the phone. "Whew. Well, that was the royal runaround. I swear I talked to five different people, but I did finally get told that *Sea Biscuit* was found and that it had been used to haul drugs." She gave Charity a thumbs up. "It'll be towed to Marsh Harbor. He said I can retrieve it when they finish processing it. Who knows? Maybe the prints they find will implicate someone later on."

As Savannah handed Charity the phone, she looked worried.

"What is it?" Charity asked.

"I feel like I just lost my chance to report Flo was kidnapped."

Charity paused. "Is that what you'd rather do? Let the police handle it? The Royal Bahamas Defence Force?"

She quickly shook her head. "No. Let's go."

The Cigarette boat pulled up alongside *Wind Dancer*, five fenders hanging from its side, evenly spaced along the rub rail. The driver, a young Bahamian man, no more than twenty years old, froze in place, his eyes

wide, when he saw the massive Rottweiler in the cockpit. Charity wasn't sure if he feared the dog or if he didn't want the hairy creature in his shiny boat.

"Mistuh Patterson din say nuttin' bout picking up a beast like dat," he said. Then he shrugged, quickly regaining his composure. "But he's di boss."

He helped Savannah and the dog aboard.

Charity tossed the few bags she'd packed to him, then turned to secure *Wind Dancer*. After she went through her usual mundane routine of locking every lock, securing all that needed to be secured, she stood in the cockpit a moment, staring at the tiny, metal mechanism. Was it an illusion of safety? Or had she willingly given up safety and security long ago when she chose this life? Was anyone truly safe? What did it matter anyway? Inside her boat was only stuff.

What mattered were the people she loved. She couldn't lock them away. As much as she wanted to protect Flo from all the evil in this world, she had a life to live. She couldn't be kept in a bubble, even though she could be taken any time, ripping Charity's heart from her chest as she went.

Somehow, in that moment, Charity knew she couldn't put a lock on her heart anymore either.

CHAPTER THIRTEEN

As soon as the boat left the harbor, turned south, and gained speed, Savannah seemed to calm. She was doing something, contributing. Charity realized Savannah had been right; staying with Henry wasn't an option. Just pacing would have killed her. If it were her own daughter who'd been kidnapped, Charity knew she certainly wouldn't be able to sit back and wait. Why should she expect Savannah to?

The wind whipped Charity's hair into a tangled mess and the twin engines roared in her ears as the boat raced across the water. She glanced at the Cigarette's speedometer; sixty miles per hour. It was chilly this time of the morning. She went down below to get warm and check the weather conditions for the flight. Luck was with them. Skies were clear from Andros Island all the way to Beaufort, South Carolina.

Two hours later, they arrived at Henry's little marina on Andros. He stood waiting for them on the dock. A man of few words, he greeted them with a nod. He understood the need for haste.

Angelique stood beside him. She lived in one of the small cabins on Henry's resort, helping him care for the guests and generally keeping the place running. The moment Savannah stepped from the boat, Angelique took her in her arms, hugging her tight. "Everyting gone be all right," she whispered. "Charity gone take care of it." When she released her from the hug, she handed her a bag. "I packed yuh some tings. Water, sandwiches. You need to take care'a yerselves now."

Savannah thanked her and quickly gave instructions on caring for Woden, his diet and usual routines. Charity thanked Angelique too, knowing she'd be the one to make sure Woden was fed, and moments later, they were in Henry's rusted old pickup on their way to the airport.

As requested, her helicopter was fueled and ready to fly.

She opened the doors to let the heat out of the black helo, while she did a thorough walkaround.

"Don't tell me you know how to fly this thing?" Savannah said, following her.

"I do. It's my helo."

She stared a moment. "Who are you, anyway?"

"I was an Army pilot. Long before we met."

Savannah leaned in and looked at the dash. "And we're going to fly all the way to Beaufort in this?" Her tone implied she didn't believe it was physically possible.

"Don't worry," Charity assured her, motioning her to get in.

Charity closed the door, went around to the pilot's seat and climbed in. She handed Savannah a set of headphones, then put on her own, as she mentally ran through her cockpit preparation flow, scanning left to right and top to bottom, confirming that all the familiar switches were at the right setting. Satisfied, she went through the startup checklist in her head and fired up the big turbine engine. It whirred to life. All sounded normal and the gauges were reading correctly. That was good. The last thing she needed right now was engine trouble on top of everything else.

Savannah's eyes traveled in awe to the overhead, then around the cockpit and across all the gauges and switches on the dash.

"Never flown in a helicopter?" Charity asked.

Savannah shook her head.

"Make sure your belt is secure, keep your hands and feet off the flight controls, and hang on," Charity said. "Keep your eyes on the horizon. The motions you'll experience will be different than on a boat." She didn't want to scare her passenger, but some people didn't have the good sense to protect against motion sickness in a bird like this, even fellow sailors. Savannah nodded her understanding.

She eased up the collective and pushed the cyclic forward. The rotors started to beat the air with a heavy whump-whump-whump, as the chopper lifted straight

up off the ground. She throttled up and the nose dropped slightly, pitching the chopper forward. As it gained speed, she climbed to a cruising altitude of 4500 feet.

The GPS showed that it was 463 air miles from San Andros Airport to Beaufort County Airport. That distance was on the edge of her fuel range. She didn't want to take any chances, so she set a course for Jacksonville, and requested a VFR flight plan with flight tracking. Miami Center gave her the squawk code and she entered it in the transponder, repeating it back to Miami.

They'd get fuel and clear customs in Jacksonville. If she wanted, Charity could fly in low, beneath the radar, direct to Beaufort, and bypass customs, but if they were detected, they'd lose a lot more time. Better to play it safe. She wanted to be in Beaufort before nightfall.

"We've got almost four hours of flight time," Charity said. "Why don't you start at the beginning. Tell me all about Derrick."

"What's to tell? He's a no-good piece of crap that I made the colossal mistake of marrying."

"You must have liked something about him at the time."

"Well, it certainly wasn't his enormous—"

Charity glanced over at her.

"—ego."

They both grinned.

Savannah's muscles clenched. Her emotions seemed to swing in an instant. "We were high school sweethearts, went to college together. It was like—" She let

out a little air. "It was like we assumed we'd be together forever, that nothing would change. Immature, I know. And then, of course, he changed."

"What happened?"

"Or maybe I changed." The tone of her voice turned softer. "Maybe I finally saw him for who he really was."

"And who was that?"

"An insecure narcissist. Everything had to be his way. Our life was all about him. And if I questioned anything, he'd lose it. I swear, he used to bait me into arguments, just so he could win. There was a time when I thought I was losing my mind. I've since learned it's called gaslighting. He would lie about things. Then when I would question him, even if I had solid proof, he had a way of making me unsure. He'd deny things so adamantly; tell me I was crazy. He wore me down.

"I swear, he had this way of blame shifting. When he'd get me guessing, he'd hit me with the word salad."

"Word salad?" Charity searched her memory. She'd never heard that term before.

"Yeah, you know, when someone isn't making any sense. He'd talk in circles. Round and round. I finally learned not to even try to follow." She pivoted in her seat to face Charity. "Maybe he was doing drugs way back then and I didn't realize."

"Could be," Charity said. "A lot of people start using in college."

"Right," Savannah said, turning forward.

"Was he a good student?"

"He was a mediocre student at best. He only passed the bar because he was knee-deep in the good-ole-boy fraternity; the fourth generation of the Coleman and Coleman law practice. Old Southern money. Now that I look back on it all, I wouldn't be surprised if Daddy had bribed the right people. One thing Derrick learned from Daddy Coleman: money is status and status is power. But his dad was the one with all the power. That was the real issue. Derrick had none. After we got married, he went to work for the firm, and that's when everything fell apart. He was at the office eighty hours a week. He couldn't take the pressure."

"He couldn't hack it as an attorney?"

"It wasn't that so much. It was his dad. That man's a tyrant. He's an unbearable, misogynistic, racist pig who expected Derrick to follow in his footsteps, which included being a misogynistic, racist pig. Mostly, he wanted Derrick to be his yes man."

"I take it you didn't like him working for his dad."

"I'll never understand why he wanted to."

"Do you think his dad is involved in the drug running?"

Savannah shook her head with confidence. "No. He might be a number-one, class-A asshole, but he's got the typical all-high-and-mighty, righteous complex. He wouldn't break the law. Not like that."

"So, it's a side gig for Derrick."

She nodded. "If it's true."

"Did you believe he was involved with drugs before this happened?"

"I heard rumors, but to be honest, I didn't care. Once I got some distance from him, I realized how messed up he truly was. I was glad to be free of him. And with the divorce, we have no legal ties. So, he can run for president or die in Colombia at the hands of some angry drug lord. It matters not a bit to me."

"What other rumors have you heard?"

"He got remarried last year."

That tidbit of information was interesting. Charity wondered what the new wife must think, if she knew of the existence of Florence.

"Did you know her?"

"Nope. Never heard of her."

"Personal habits?" Charity asked.

"The only thing I know for sure is he still works for his dad. But I'd bet that he still goes to the gym three days a week. He was obsessive about it. And he probably still hangs out at this crappy old biker bar out on the edge of town with his old high school buddies. I can't think of the name. Hey—" Her eyes lit up. "Maybe Donny hangs out there, and—"

Charity was right with her. "And maybe that's where his drug business is headquartered. Maybe his old buddies are his dealers? Or at least his muscle." Charity started to descend to land in Jacksonville.

"Quick stop, and we'll be back in the air," she said.

Jacksonville was a high traffic area, which was, in some ways, an advantage. They were able to breeze through customs and use the bathroom while the ground crew refueled the bird. Less than forty minutes after landing, they were given clearance to take off again without incident.

Once back in the air, Charity asked Savannah to pass her one of the sandwiches Angelique had packed for them. It was so like that woman to think of these things. She'd cared for Moana and Fiona without a moment's hesitation when Charity had asked, taking them shopping for decent clothes and showing them what real, unconditional love felt like. And now, she was still looking out for those in need. That woman had such a big heart. Charity had taken that for granted, she now realized, and vowed that when she got back to Andros, she would tell her how much she appreciated her.

Savannah peeled back the baggie so Charity could keep the sandwich in the bag while she held it.

Charity swung her boom mic up to her forehead and took a bite, chewing slowly as she considered how to express her next idea. When she lowered the mic back down, she said, "I've been thinking. Maybe, when we get to Beaufort, you should go to your mom's place. And keep hidden. You'll be right there to help when I need you, but—"

Savannah jerked back, glaring at her. "Are you kidding? I can't tell my mom. She'll die of fright. No. And I already told you, I'm not going to sit around and

wait. I'm going after Derrick. As soon as we find Flo, I'm going to wring his neck with my bare hands."

That's just what I'm afraid of, Charity thought. She tried to let it go, but her nerves were on edge. So much so, that when she went to take another bite from the sandwich, she nearly stuffed the boom mic into her mouth.

She couldn't blame Savannah. She'd feel exactly the same way. The problem was, she wasn't confident that Savannah could control the impulse when she needed to. Right now, she was an emotional wild card. Charity would have to watch her carefully. She didn't need a liability.

Her phone beeped with an incoming message. It was from Chyrel, all the info she could find on Derrick and Donny. She handed the phone to Savannah to go through the reports, reading aloud what little was in them that they didn't already know, and speed mumbling through the parts they did. Derrick's new wife's name was Annabelle. He still worked at his father's firm. He had a clean record. Donny, on the other hand, had had a few brushes with the law. Bar fights, mainly. He'd worked as a shrimper since high school. His tax returns put him just above poverty level.

When they finally landed at the Beaufort County airport on Lady's Island, it was after eight p.m. local time. The sun cast a golden light on the hangars. When Savannah exited the aircraft, heading straight for the restroom, Charity got up from her seat and popped open the floor panel in the back of the Huey. On the starboard

bulkhead was a hidden release catch, rigged courtesy of her former boss, Travis Stockwell, head of the Caribbean Counterterrorism Command. When she flipped the catch, the edge of the storage box popped up. Once she removed the box, she could access a hidden compartment below and the firearms she had stashed there. She had her father's Colt 1911, but she wanted a backup. She chose the Sig Sauer P229, placed it in her backpack, then quickly replaced the box, threw her backpack over her shoulder, and headed for the hangar. She had to use the restroom, too.

No one was at the desk. Charity had to fill out a form to register to leave her chopper and get it refueled while they were in town and she dropped the form in a box. Luckily, Chyrel had arranged for a rental car for them. The keys lay on the desk with a note attached.

"Big city service," Charity said with a little sarcasm.

"Welcome to Frogmore International Airport," Savannah responded with a grin.

"Frogmore?"

"It's a little town out on Saint Helena Island, the next island toward the coast. Home of Frogmore stew."

"I don't even want to know what's in that," Charity said, as they went out to the parking lot.

The two of them set out for their first stakeout—Derrick's house. The odds that he had Flo there were slim, but Donny was probably already out shrimping for the night, and they had to start somewhere. Charity just wanted to

take a look. You never knew where you might get a clue, and his house was as good a place to start as any.

Savannah gave directions as Charity drove the plain, nondescript four-door sedan from the airport to an area Savannah called New Point.

"Why is it called New Point?" Charity asked, as she turned off of Sam's Point Road.

"The Point is the most desired neighborhood in Beaufort," Savannah said. "It's just across the river in the old historic part of town. That's where Derrick's dad lives. New Point was built for yuppies. I hate it."

It was dark as they drove down his street. The old-style streetlights had come on and the houses' windows glowed a warm amber.

"We're not going to be able to sit on the street in the car for long without drawing suspicion," Charity said as she rolled to a stop in front of Derrick's house. No lights were on inside.

The place looked like a re-creation of a civil war-era mansion, but smaller, designed for the likes of Scarlett O' Hara's great-great-granddaughter, with perfectly manicured landscaping. Quite pretentious. Charity couldn't picture Savannah living there. "Did you live here with him or is this new?"

"It was our house. I hated it. Marriage is all about compromises though, right?" She said it with a smirk. "Like I said, it was all about him. He wanted a house in New Point, so he could look across the river to where his dad lives."

They didn't have to wait long. A gray Jaguar XJ turned down the street and pulled into the driveway.

"He always wanted that stupid car," Savannah mumbled. "Jackass."

The garage door went up, he pulled into the garage, and the door slowly closed behind him.

"The house is dark. Nobody's home. I'm thinking that—"

"Good," Savannah said. "Now's our chance." The car door was flung open and the overhead light came on.

Charity seized her by the wrist. "Whoa, whoa, whoa." She yanked her back into the seat. "What do you think you're doing?"

"He's going to tell me where she is or I'm going to kill him." Charity could see her clearly now that the dome light was on. Her face was flushed. She'd been getting more worked up than Charity had realized.

Dammit. She should have been paying closer attention. Charity quickly doused the light. If Derrick got a glimpse of Savannah, it'd be all over. "He's not going to tell you anything," she stated emphatically. "If you go in there like a pissed-off she-bear after her cub, all you'll do is tip him off. What do you think he'll do then? He'll probably move her, and this time, to a place we'll never find her. Do you understand that?"

Savannah turned to face her, eyes on fire. Charity felt bad scaring her, but she couldn't have her blowing the one advantage they had.

"Right now," Charity said, softening her tone, "he thinks he's got the upper hand. Our best advantage is for him to think you're dead."

Savannah clenched her teeth together.

"You have to trust me," Charity said. "We talked about this."

Savannah huffed and slammed the door.

Charity put the car in gear and pressed on the gas before Savannah could change her mind. "Besides, I was just about to say, I have a theory."

"What theory?"

"Well, it's 9:30 at night."

"So?"

"So, where's the new wife?"

"I don't know. Who cares?"

"We do. Because I'll bet you dollars to donuts, wherever she is, Flo's with her."

Savannah sat back in the seat. "I hadn't thought about that."

Charity relaxed. "I know."

She started sniffling. "I'm sorry."

"Remember when I said—"

"I know. I know. God, I'm stupid."

"You're not stupid. You're upset. You're in an emotional turmoil. I know that, I get it. For me, when that happens, I have to let someone else call the shots."

Savannah looked over at Charity. "I don't believe you."

"I don't know why you'd—"

"I don't believe you're ever in a position that you're not in complete control."

Charity stared straight ahead. It was true. On the job, emotion was unacceptable. She'd tamp down any tiny hint of a feeling into the deep recesses of her being. But she'd paid a big price. She'd often wondered if she'd ever truly feel anything again.

They found the Airbnb that Chyrel had rented for them, a small two-bedroom apartment over a huge garage just a mile from New Point. The best part was, there was a restaurant just down the street. A place called Dockside. It looked like it was closing when they'd driven past, but if they were there for any length of time, it was good to know where to get food.

Charity encouraged Savannah to get to bed, get some sleep, but she might as well have asked the moon to rise in the west.

"I'm sorry, Charity. I promise, whatever you say, I'll do. I swear it. It won't happen again."

Charity nodded. She didn't like having to treat Savannah like a subordinate, but she couldn't let her go off all half-cocked and blow everything. This was too important.

"It's just that, when I saw him, you know..." Savannah collapsed into the couch. "I never thanked you for saving my life. I mean it. Thank you. If you hadn't been there..."

"I was. And I'm glad. I'd do it again."

"I know. I just need to say thank you."

Charity gave her a gentle smile.

"And helping find Flo. I don't know what I'd do. This whole nightmare, it's too much."

"We're going to tackle it together. Me and you. We're going to find Flo. We're going to get her back. Do you hear me? We're going to get her back."

Savannah looked into Charity's eyes. "Are you trying to convince me or yourself?"

Charity held her gaze. "Failure is not an option."

CHAPTER FOURTEEN

Flo stared out the bedroom window at the ocean. The woman had said that the man who'd left was her father, and she needed to start treating him with respect. But she didn't have a father.

Yet, that wasn't exactly true. Everyone had a father. It took a man and woman to make a baby. She knew that. Which meant she had a father—somewhere. So, could it be true? Was that guy really her father?

It didn't make sense. Why hadn't her mother told her about him?

She wiped a tear from her eye. She didn't know what to believe. She just wanted to go home, back to her boat, and her dog. And find out if her mom was still alive.

Could she really be dead?

Her tummy ached and her mouth was dry. This was all too scary. She wrapped her arms around her chest, hugging herself, and rocked back and forth.

Maybe her mom was dead. The image of her floating face down in the water kept popping into Flo's mind.

No, she couldn't be. If she were, Flo knew that she would somehow know it, feel it.

This wasn't real. None of it. It was like a movie she'd watched once, where the girl was having a bad dream. That was it. She was having a bad dream and she was going to wake up any time now. Then it would be over, and she'd be back with her mom. Her real mom. Not this crazy woman who smelled like too much perfume and kept telling her to call her mom.

She squeezed her eyes closed, trying not to cry.

Her real dad was a good man. Her mom had said so. The guy who was here last night couldn't be her dad. He was awful. But what if he was? What if the man her mom had described was just who she'd wanted the father of her child to be? She had a father. Somewhere.

Flo wasn't stupid. She knew about divorce. Some people got married and then couldn't get along. Her grandma had told her about that. Maybe that's what had happened with her mom and dad. Maybe she just didn't want him around?

One day, when she was little, she and her mom were watching a male osprey bringing food to his mate, sitting on the nest. *See the daddy osprey taking food to the mommy and babies?* her mom had said.

What's a daddy? she'd asked. That's when her mom had explained how it takes a man and a woman together to make a baby. But the man didn't always need to stay to help, like with ospreys. She and her mom were just fine, just the two of them, on their own.

Flo hadn't liked that answer. She wanted a dad. And when she'd learned she had one, somewhere out there in the world, she'd wanted to meet him.

The timing has just never been right, her mom had said.

Doesn't he want to meet me? she'd asked.

Her mom had stared at her. *He doesn't know about you,* she'd finally admitted. *I've wanted to tell him, but I couldn't.*

She didn't understand. Why wouldn't her mom tell her dad about her? Why? She'd stormed off and hid in her room. Through the overhead hatch she'd heard her mom sobbing up on the bridge. She'd never forget that night. It was the first time she'd ever known her mom to cry.

Flo had gone to her and hugged her and told her she was sorry.

I'm the one who's sorry, her mom had said. *It was my choice. I've done what I thought was best.* She told Flo about her father then, how he was a fine and decent man, a man of the sea, free as a bird, and how some birds wanted to fly around, not stay in one place. And that was okay.

Then she remembered what else her mom had said that night. That one day she'd get to meet him. Was this that day? She had dreamed about it, but not like this. Her dreams were nothing like this. He was supposed to be kind and bring her gifts and make her mom smile.

No, this Derrick guy couldn't be her father. He couldn't be the man her mom said she'd meet one day.

None of this felt right. And her mom always said, if something didn't feel right, to trust her gut. And her gut wasn't feeling very good. It was all in knots.

Derrick had left and Flo was glad. He'd made it very clear that she was trapped here. She couldn't leave the house, even to go outside, or she'd be in big trouble. He'd hit her with the belt.

She had to figure out what to do.

Her mom had told her once, knowledge is power. She needed to know if this Derrick was really her father and if her mom was really dead. Then she'd figure out what to do.

The woman wasn't so bad. Maybe if she talked to her, she could find out the truth. If Derrick was really her father, he'd know where she was born and other stuff. She got up from the chair and went downstairs to the living room. The woman was sitting on the couch.

"There you are, dear," she said, looking up from a book. "Are you feeling better? Are you hungry?"

"Yes, ma'am."

A cell phone sat on the end table. Flo's nerves tingled all over her body. She hadn't thought of that. She could try to call her mom. Her mom would have her phone with her, like when grandma was going to call from the hospital. Mom had carried the phone with her everywhere until she'd called.

That's what she'd do. But she was sure this woman wasn't going to let her use her phone. She'd have to find a way to get to the phone without her knowing.

The woman set the book down, rose from the couch, then grabbed the phone and shoved it into her back pocket before heading for the kitchen. "What do you like? A grilled cheese sandwich?"

"Sure. Thank you."

"Do you want some milk with it?"

"No, thank you." She hadn't drunk milk since she was a little kid. "What's your name?"

The woman paused, smiled. This seemed to delight her. "You can call me Anna, if you want. But some day I'm hoping you'll call me Mom."

That's never going to happen, crazy lady.

She took a loaf of bread and a tub of butter from the refrigerator.

Maybe there was another phone. Her grandma had one that was plugged into the wall. Maybe there was one like that here. Or a computer. If her mom was really dead, it would be on the internet. When her aunt had died, there was a post on the internet. She couldn't remember what it was called. A special death post. It started with an O. That was the answer. She needed to find out. That's how she'd know for sure. She needed to get on the internet. But first, she needed to find out if there was a computer in this house. "I need to go to the bathroom."

Anna held a piece of bread and started spreading butter on it. "Of course."

Flo headed back upstairs and down the hall, but she went right past the bathroom. There was one more room

further down. She pushed the door open and poked her head in. There was nothing but a big bed with a flowery bedspread, a bedside table with a lamp, a dresser, and a couple of suitcases. No phone. No computer. She went into the room and checked inside the suitcases. No laptop in there.

The room was weird. It reminded her of the hotel she and her mom had stayed at once. There was nothing personal in it. Nothing on the dresser except for a dusty, fake flower arrangement. She peeked in the closet. Only two shirts and one dress hung there.

Anna didn't live here. Maybe this was one of those oceanside rental houses where tourists stayed for a week or two. But why would they be at a rental house?

She went back to the kitchen and sat down on a stool at the bar counter. Anna stood at the stove, flipping her sandwich in the pan. The phone was in her back pocket. Still. How was she going to get it?

Her sandwich was done. Anna slid it onto a paper plate and set it down in front of Flo. "How about a Coke?"

"I'm not allowed to drink soda."

"Oh."

Flo liked the look on Anna's face. "You can have one, though. I won't tell Derrick."

Anna looked confused. "Well, I've already eaten. I didn't know you were going to join me. You seemed too upset."

Flo picked up the sandwich and took a bite. It was actually pretty good. She was hungry.

"What do you like to do?" Anna asked. "Do you like to go swimming? I bet you're a good swimmer. I bought you a brand-new swimsuit."

She thought of Charity and her swim lessons, and clamped her mouth shut. Then the tears came.

"Oh, there, there, darling. Don't cry." Anna came around the counter and put her arm around Flo.

Flo yanked free of her. "Leave me alone."

"Okay, all right. I just want you to be happy. We can do anything you want to do today. You decide."

"I want to go see my mom."

"We can't do that."

Flo stared into her eyes. "Is it because she's dead?"

"What?" Anna stepped back. "Why would you say that?"

"I saw her. She tried to save me so they killed her. They left her in the water to drown."

Anna looked pale. She shook her head. "That's not true."

"It is true. I saw her in the water." She threw the sandwich down on the counter and ran back up to her room and buried her head in the fluffy pillows.

Anna came to the door. "Don't cry. I'm sure it's not what you think. You know how sometimes we see things and we misunderstand what's happened? I'm sure that's what's going on now."

Flo wouldn't look up at her.

"How about we go build a sandcastle?"

"No."

"You can't stay in this room with your head buried forever."

"Leave me alone."

She sat down on the edge of the bed. "I don't think that's a good idea. I want you to sit up and put a smile on your face."

"How can I smile when my mom might be dead?"

"She's not dead."

Then why doesn't she come get me? This was so confusing. She sat up. "You're lying. She'd come get me."

"Your mom's in custody. She's going to jail."

"No, she's not."

"Florence, listen to me—"

"How do you know my name?"

"I know lots of things about you."

"Like what?"

"I know you and your mom lived on a boat called *Sea Biscuit* that your grandpa rebuilt for you."

"Everybody knows that."

"I know your birthday is July 13."

Flo stared at her. How'd she know that?

"I know you love your mom, but you're going to have to accept that you live with me now."

She couldn't breathe. She didn't want to live with Anna and Derrick. "I won't."

"You'll have to." She said the words like there was no other option. "Because your mom is going to jail for a long time."

"But my mom didn't do anything wrong."

"She did. You'll have to accept that, too."

No, I won't. Not just because this stranger said so. She had to find out for herself. If her mom was alive, or if she was in jail. She needed a computer.

She nodded, acting like she was giving in.

"That's a good girl. Now, what shall we do that's fun?"

"I have homework to do." That would get her a computer.

"No, not now. Forget about that. There'll be time later for school. Let's do something fun."

"But I'll fall behind. I need a computer so I can do my homework."

"Well, we don't have one here. So, how about you don't worry about that right now. You want to build a sandcastle?"

"Sandcastles are for babies. I'm not five." She flopped on her side and pulled another pillow over her head.

Anna sighed and got up from the bed. "Suit yourself."

A few minutes later, Flo heard Anna's footsteps, padding down the hall and into the bathroom. Then the shower water was running. She wouldn't take her phone into the shower with her. This was her chance to call her mom.

Flo leapt from the bed and scurried down the hall. The door was unlocked. She pushed it open an inch and peeked in. The phone was on the vanity top. She pushed the door open a little farther and carefully stepped toward it. She had it— the phone was in her

hand. Anna was splashing water around in the shower, and Flo froze. What would she do if Anna caught her?

She had to find out, no matter what. She clicked the button to turn on the screen, but it required a passcode, and Flo had no idea what it could be. All her courage evaporated, and tears welled up in her eyes. She set the phone back down, exactly where she'd found it, and retreated to the bedroom and back under the pillows. Now what was she going to do?

The shower shut off and within minutes, Anna was dressed and standing at her doorway. "Have you changed your mind? Is there anything you'd like to do today?"

The buzz of a boat engine coming toward the house got her attention. She went to the window. Flo followed. A skiff was pulling up to the dock.

"You stay here," Anna said with a stern voice, and went out the door. The phone was back in her pocket.

Flo watched from the window as Anna went down the stairs and out onto the dock. A man in the boat placed several bags on the dock. They looked like grocery bags. He gestured toward the house, but Anna shook her head. She paid him cash and he gestured toward the house again. He must have been offering to carry the bags for her, but Anna declined. She picked up three bags and headed toward the house. The skiff left the dock and sped away.

When Anna came through the door, she called for Flo. Flo came out of her room and down the stairs.

"Would you please go get the rest of those bags?"

"I thought you said I had to stay in the house."

The woman gave her an exasperated frown. "You can go right now. Just to get the bags."

"Okay." Flo went out the sliding door, across the porch, and down the stairs. As she did, she scanned the surrounding area. To the left, which she was sure was north, she could see the very top of a lighthouse. It had one red and one white stripe above the trees. That was the Hope Town Lighthouse. She was sure of it. And across the channel and a little south was Tahiti Beach. She and her mom had stopped there one day for a picnic. She knew where she was. She was on Lubber's Quarters Cay.

Now she knew what to do.

She grabbed the two remaining bags of groceries and headed back inside the house. She had a plan. All she had to do was figure out the right time.

Anna was putting away the groceries from the first three bags. "If you'll tell me what you like to eat, I can place another order from the grocery store. Whatever you want. We'll get all your favorites."

"I'm not going to be staying that long," Flo said and headed back to her room.

Behind her, she heard Anna slam whatever she'd been holding down on the counter.

"Come back here, young lady."

She came to a halt and spun around. "What are you going to do? Ground me?" She turned and continued to her room.

CHAPTER FIFTEEN

Donny McLaughlin was a shrimper and shrimp were nocturnal creatures, foraging the bottom at night. That meant Donny worked nights and would return to port around dawn.

Charity convinced Savannah to stay at the Airbnb while she went down to the 11th Street pier in Port Royal, where all the shrimp boats made port, to take a look around.

It was early. The sun was barely hinting at its arrival. As Charity walked along the docks, a low fog rolled in off the sound. She drew in a deep breath, missing *Wind Dancer* and the peace of floating on the sea.

Flo's pixie face flashed into her mind, smiling with joy as she dove from the back of *Sea Biscuit*. Charity's stomach clenched as a thought struck her: maybe Derrick had nothing to do with it. The only connection they'd made between Donny and Flo was Derrick. But Savannah was from Beaufort. She could have other enemies here. There could be other connections, other motives.

Charity immediately dismissed her doubts. The scenario they'd arrived at made perfect sense. Derrick had motive, opportunity, and, as Savannah had described, all the anger and desire to do something so rotten. Donny was his stooge. He was the key to confirmation about Derrick's involvement and any information as to Flo's whereabouts.

If she could find him, she'd get it out of him.

From what she knew about shrimpers, they were elusive creatures. Sometimes they went out on their boats to work, sometimes not. Their whims seemed more capricious than weather dependent.

Probably depended on the severity of the hangover, she thought. Whatever the reasons, they weren't the type of men who punched time clocks.

She found a bench with a view of the entire marina and sat down. This might take a while, and time was one thing they didn't have. Savannah was a ticking time bomb, and though she had promised to behave, there was no telling when she might blow.

As for Flo, Charity had no idea how she might be handling all of this. But there wasn't a damned thing she could do about it anyway. Right now, she could only wait.

She'd been trained to wait, to be patient. She'd spent more than one night sitting in a patrol car, staking out some lowlife's crib. With DHS, she'd learned to set up ambushes and infiltrate an enemy camp. These operations required more than patience. They required steel nerves. But she'd never had a cherished little girl de-

pending on her, held in conditions she didn't want to ponder.

She looked out toward the vast sound and the ocean beyond. *Donny, don't make me hunt you like a dog. The longer it takes, the angrier I'll get.*

As if on cue, a shrimp boat, with its distinctive outriggers, appeared out of the fog, just turning into the river or creek where the marina was located. It was heading toward the docks. She rose from the bench and casually strolled down the dock, timing her pace so she could get a good look at the crew as they tied up.

Three men were aboard. Donny wasn't among them. She decided to take a chance.

"Good morning," she said.

One of the men raised his head and mumbled a good morning back as he secured a dock line to a cleat.

"I'm looking for Donny. Donny McLaughlin. Know him?"

"Yeah."

"Know where I can find him?"

The man, encased in a yellow slicker, his sopping wet beard hanging out under the hood, turned to his crew mate. "You seen Donny?"

Charity added, "He's an old friend."

The shipmate, looking much like the first guy, except that his jacket was green, pointed at a shrimp boat docked two slips down. "Already in for the day."

"Ah, thanks," she said. "Know where I might find him now?" She had his home address, but if she didn't find him there, she needed other options.

The man shrugged. The first guy thought about it a moment. "Maybe over at Cry Babies?"

"Yeah, probably," the second added. "Good breakfast."

"Thanks, I appreciate it." She walked down the dock to get a look at the trawler they'd claimed he worked on. Scrawled across the bow was the name *Hustler*. Very fitting.

As she headed for her car, she dialed the number for the phone at the Airbnb. She thought she'd let Savannah know where she was headed, that she might be there a while, waiting on Donny if she didn't find him at home, but she also wanted to confirm Savannah had stayed put as she'd promised.

Savannah answered; her voice anxious. "Did you find him?"

"Not yet. I found out what boat he's on and that he likes to frequent a certain breakfast place. Cry Babies. I'm going there now."

"That's it. Cry Babies. That's the old biker bar I told you about."

"Good," Charity said.

"What can I do? I'm pacing a damned hole in the carpet."

"I know." She thought a moment. "You know, if you could do some research, that would help a lot. Fire up my laptop. See if Donny has a Facebook account. Let's

look at what he's been up to, make a list of all the places he's been lately. That'll help me find him much quicker."

"Got it. I'm on it." She disconnected.

Charity doubted the man had a Facebook account. If he did, Chyrel would have found it. She doubted he owned a computer or, for that matter, had ever touched one, but Savannah needed the distraction.

She got back in the rental car, found the address for the restaurant on her phone, tapped *Directions*, and pulled out of the parking lot.

Cry Babies was about six miles away. His house was closer, so she made a quick pass on the way. No one was home. If Donny was a regular at this Cry Babies place, it was likely he or Derrick, or both of them were moving drugs out of the bar. That's where she needed to be.

Cry Babies was a flat-roofed shack with a solid steel door at the entrance, the paint peeling away in big chunks. A row of rusted barrels leaned against the wall. Several old pickups were randomly parked in the gravel lot.

Charity paused before entering. She was going to stand out. Her hair needed to be greasier. Her shirt should have a beer logo or something. But she didn't have time. She'd have to wing it. She left her weapon and tactical bag in the car. If she was going to draw attention, scrutinization usually followed.

As she stepped inside, the odor of decades-old cigarette tar, stale deep-fryer grease, and the distinctly pungent smell of fishermen's boots hit her in the face.

She paused a moment to let her nose recover and her eyes adjust to the darkness. There was one window on the far wall, overlooking the marsh. A bar ran the full length of the wall to her left. Some of the stools were occupied by fishermen, just in from the sea. In the other direction, a back room held a pool table.

She moved to take a table where her back would be to the window and she'd have a view of the entire place to watch for Donny.

A waitress, older than her mother would have been, her hair pulled back with bobby pins, shuffled toward her. Her name tag read *Ethel*. In the raspy voice of a chain smoker, she said, "What can I gitcha, sweetheart?"

"I heard you have a fantastic breakfast."

The woman looked amused. "Our special today is the Old Timer's plate. Four eggs, two sausage, two bacon, hash browns, and toast or grits."

"Sounds great," Charity said. "With coffee."

"Toast or grits?"

"Toast, please."

She shuffled away.

Charity clicked through her phone to look at Donny's picture one more time, then scanned the occupants of the restaurant once again. All men. Donny wasn't among them.

Ethel was back with a cup of coffee. "Cream or sugar?"

"No, thanks. Black's fine."

She took a sip of the rotgut brew and the flavor instantly took her back to flight school. At the time, she

was sure they served crappy coffee as some kind of punishment or the Army's way of saying *Buck up, life isn't a bed of roses*. But it never got any better. Same at the Starbucks on base in Afghanistan. The brew they served would burn a hole through the bottom of your stomach.

When Ethel arrived with a platter piled with food and plopped it in front of Charity, she was still contemplating how long she could get away with hanging out, waiting to see if Donny showed.

"It will take me all day to eat all that food," she said.

Ethel shrugged. "We ain't exactly got em' lining up outside waiting to get in."

She left but came right back with the coffee pot to refill Charity's cup. "We got Tums for sale at the counter if you need it."

Charity wasn't sure if she was serious.

She picked up her fork, and, out of habit, gave a quick inspection. One tine was bent. She wasn't surprised. At least it was clean. After three bites, the door swung open. Sunlight gushed in, temporarily blinding everyone inside. It was Donny. He went straight to the bar. Ethel met him with a cup of coffee.

He was a big man, tall and husky. Bigger than Charity had estimated from his picture. It didn't worry her. It was simply an observation. In her experience, the bigger the man, the less fighting skill they usually possessed. Big men went through life winning fights by intimidation. She'd be cautious just the same.

A straight-up confrontation here might not be the best approach anyway. This was going to take a little finesse. She needed to get him outside alone.

He wasn't exactly the kind of guy most women found attractive. If she made a pass at him, he might suspect something was off right away. She needed something else to get close. Now she wished she would have taken a seat at the bar.

Ethel stopped back by her table with an obligatory "Everything good?"

"A pleasant surprise," she said, and she meant it. The bacon was crispy. The sausages had just the right spices. Even the eggs were cooked to perfection. Now, she regretted not ordering the grits. "My compliments to the chef."

Ethel smirked as she walked away.

Charity slowly devoured the entire platter while she waited for Donny to finish his breakfast. As soon as he took the last bite, he wiped his mouth with a paper napkin, dropped it on the plate in front of him, grabbed his mug of coffee, and headed for the back room. Another man, who had been sitting three bar stools down, did the same, following Donny.

Were they going to play pool? She didn't have a good view from her table. She got up and headed for the lady's room, an excuse to peek in. Sure enough, Donny was racking up the balls.

She quickly used the bathroom and paid her bill, making sure to give Ethel an extra-generous tip. She

paused, amused, when she saw the rolls of Tums in the glass case under the cash register.

With two quarters in her hand, she went into the back room and placed them on the rail of the pool table, indicating she'd like to play the winner. Donny and the other man, another shrimper, she assumed, with similar build and the same dirty beard, exchanged an amused look.

"Well, who have we here?" the other man said.

"Gabby," Charity replied, falling easily into the persona of her alias, Gabriela Fleming. "Who are you?"

"Ben." He gestured toward Donny with his cue stick. "This here's Donny."

Donny nodded.

Charity crawled onto a bar stool in the corner and watched as they resumed their game of eight ball. One thing about guys like this, they didn't ask a lot of questions.

Ben hit every ball with the same amount of force, as hard as he could, sending balls ricocheting all over the table. But Donny had some skills. She hoped he would win for two reasons: first, he was her target and second, Ben was going to drive her nuts. The man had no subtlety.

Finally, Donny sank the two-ball, the last of the solids, then strutted around the table to line up for the eight-ball.

His aim was good— the eight-ball dropped in the pocket, but the cue ball kept rolling, rolling, rolling.

Oh, please don't scratch, she thought. It teetered on the edge of the pocket but didn't drop in. She let out her breath as she rose from the stool, clapping her hands. "Bravo."

Without a word, Ben handed his cue stick to Charity. "Show 'em how it's done," he said.

Donny dropped the quarters in the coin slot, then shoved it in, and the balls dropped with a clatter. He placed the ball rack on the table and started arranging the balls.

"Money breaks," he said.

"It's been a while," Charity said. "But I think I can hold my own."

Donny gave no response. Once the balls were set, he carefully removed the rack. "Have at it."

She set the cue ball on the table, slightly to the right of center, lined up, and with practiced precision, hit the one ball straight on, scattering the balls all over the table. Two of them dropped into pockets.

"Impressive," Ben said, grinning. "Two stripes."

"It's like riding a bike, I guess," she said. It was true. She hadn't played in a while, but in Afghanistan, she'd put in a lot of hours running the table in the O-club.

As she chose her next shot, she was acutely aware of the view the angle of her body would provide as she leaned over the table. She knew it wouldn't take much to get Donny's mind right where she wanted it. She made a bank shot and sank the twelve-ball.

"Nice!" Ben said with a snicker.

She had to be careful. Donny might run off with his tail between his legs if she beat him. She took another shot, sank the nine-ball, but let the cue ball follow into the pocket for a scratch.

"Darn it," she said. "Your shot."

After making a show of swizzling chalk onto the tip of his cue, creating a tiny blue cloud that lingered after he walked away, Donny sank two of his balls, then he missed the third, an easy cut shot.

Charity sank another one with a kick shot off the far rail, but then faked a miss cue, added a giggle for effect, and conceded that maybe she was a little rusty.

Donny smirked. As he came around the other side of the table, she could swear she saw his knuckles dragging.

A couple more men came into the back room. At first, she thought they'd want to play next and she'd have to move fast on Donny, but they leaned against the wall, watching. Then, a few minutes later, a few more men arrived. It seemed a woman playing pool was a spectacle they wanted to witness.

She let Donny win the first game. He gave Ben a high five. Charity shook her head. This idiot probably didn't get laid much. She dug two more quarters from her pocket. "Another one?"

His bushy eyebrows shot up. "That wasn't enough for yah?"

"I'm just getting warmed up." She dropped the coins in the slot. "What do you say we put some money on it?"

He shook his head. "Can't. We'll get kicked out." He pointed to a sign on the wall that read *No Gambling*.

She leaned toward him to whisper in his ear, "Just between you and me. Three out of five, loser buys the beer."

The side of his mouth curled up into a half grin.

During the fifth game, after quite a crowd had gathered, and Charity was getting really good at holding their attention simply by bending over, a new guy showed up in the room. He was younger than the others, dressed in jeans and a T-shirt. He wasn't a shrimper. Looked like a college kid who'd wandered off campus, lost.

He got Donny's attention. Donny handed his cue to Ben. "Stand in for me, will yah? I'll be right back."

Ben gladly took the stick, but Charity wasn't happy about it. "Hey, we got a bet going here."

Donny smirked. "You know he ain't worth a shit. You got the advantage. I'll be right back."

She followed him, far enough to reposition herself to see where he went. The men's room. Great.

As Ben took his time assessing the table, she listened for the men's room door. Ben missed his shot. She approached, chose a difficult bank shot. When she missed, the men cawed at her. She moved back to where she had a view of the men's room door. It opened. The two came out. The young kid had his hands in his pockets. No doubt there was a little green baggie of ecstasy in there.

Donny came right back to the game, snatched his cue from Ben, and walked around the table, his eyes on the balls.

"You were right," Charity said. "About Ben."

Ben blushed and the other men razzed him with guffaws.

When they finally finished the fifth game, Charity, having won, followed Donny to the bar, reminding him he owed her a beer.

"Kinda early, ain't it?" he said.

"What's your point? You trying to get out of it?" She smiled at him.

"Nah."

She leaned in close. "Unless you got more of whatever it was you sold that kid?"

He jerked back. "What? I didn't sell him nothing."

"Uh-huh." She gave him her best lusty eyes. "Right."

He stared back; mouth open. What a meathead.

"We can forget the beer and hang out somewhere," she said. "Somewhere else."

"Yeah, where?"

"I dunno. You got a place?"

"I dunno."

I should just club him in the head and get it over with.

"Listen, we're cool and all. I'm just trying to score some X. I heard, maybe, I dunno, you might have some."

"What'd you hear?" He snorted, snuffling in some phlegm.

You're such a catch. "I heard maybe you could hook me up."

"You a cop?"

"No. But isn't that what a cop would say?"

He thought about that for a moment. "Yeah. I guess you're right."

"How about just one? What could it hurt? You owe me a beer anyway."

"That's true."

"Let's go out back," she suggested.

He nodded and headed for the door.

She followed him out and around the building to a spot near the edge of the marsh under a huge live oak. It was low-tide, and the smell of the exposed mud was nasty. Charity knew not to comment on the stink. Donny might peg her as a non-local and be suspicious.

"I got some new stuff," he said, as he dug in his pocket and pulled out a baggie. A green baggie with yellow tape. Just like the ones planted on Savannah's boat. He dipped his dirty fingers into the bag and handed her one tablet. It was light pink with an imprint of a bunny on it, like a child's vitamin. That alone made her want to wring his neck on the spot. What if a kid got hold of one of those? Or worse, the whole bag?

"Aren't you going to do some, too?" She gave him her best demure smile.

He eyed her as though it was the first moment he'd noticed she was female and might be interested in him.

"Why not?" The grubby fingers rummaged around in the baggie again.

He pulled out another pink tablet and popped it into his mouth.

She faked popping hers in as well, made a big act of swallowing, and pocketed the pill. Then she sat down on the ground next to the tree. He sat next to her and they stared out over the marsh toward another island on the other side for a few minutes, long enough for the drug to kick in.

"This is some good stuff," Charity said, leaning back on the tree. "Wow."

"I told you," he said.

"Omigod, that is the most amazing tree I've ever seen." She stroked the bark. "It's alive, I swear. I just want to pet it."

"I want to pet you," he said, reaching for her hair.

She grabbed him by the wrist. "Not so fast, Donny boy."

His eyes slowly grew wide. He wasn't keeping up. Good.

"Where do you get this stuff, anyway? It's dee-vine."

"I got a source."

"Uh-huh. How do I get more?"

He tapped her on the chest with his index finger. "Anytime you want, baby."

She leaned close, just to watch his eyes refocus. He was definitely feeling the effects. "Yeah? Are you, like, the kingpin of Port Royal?"

A smile slowly formed on his lips. "Yeah. Yeah, that's it. The kingpin."

She leaned in close again, testing his vision.

He had to pull back a little to focus. "You have the most bee-oo-tiful eyes. They're like...pinwheels."

"Thanks. But, uh, I need you to focus. I got a question for you."

"What?" He stuck his finger in his ear and shook it as if he was trying to scratch the inside of his head.

She seized him by the wrist, cranked his arm back, and pinned him to the tree. "Two days ago, you kidnapped a little girl. Where is she?"

"What? What the hell, woman!"

She twisted his wrist a little harder.

He let out a squeal that sounded like it came from an infant.

"Talk."

"I don't know what you're—"

Charity twisted until she knew the tendons were stretching beyond their natural length. "I said talk."

"Yeah, yeah. I did. So what? What's it to you?"

"See, that doesn't matter. You need to focus, Donny. Use your head. What matters is I'm going to rip your arm off at the shoulder and beat you with it, if you don't tell me where she is."

He winced. "I don't know."

"Wrong answer." She twisted some more.

"I was on the grab team," he said through clenched teeth. "That was it." His head fell back and his mouth dropped open, but he didn't let out a sound.

"The grab team? What does that mean?" She knew, but she wanted him to keep talking.

He grinned, staring up at the tree's canopy. The dumbass. "It means I grabbed her."

"Funny. Then what happened? What'd you do with her?"

"Nothing. Dropped her off, man. I ain't no babysitter." He lowered his gaze, looked in her eyes. "Now let go of my arm."

"Fine." She let go and grabbed his other wrist, gave it a twist and slammed his elbow into the tree. "Donny, don't disappoint me. What do you mean, you dropped her off? Where?"

His neck was turning red, but his face was white. Apparently, the ecstasy wasn't masking everything. "I passed her on. That's how it works."

"You're making this more difficult than it has to be." She put more pressure on the elbow. "Where is she now?"

His eyes locked on hers. "How the hell should I know?" He closed his eyes again.

She pounced, ramming her knee into his groin, and seized him by the neck. "You think I'm messing around?" She applied just the right amount of pressure on his trachea, knowing the pain would slice right through his fog-addled brain. "Who hired you? Was it Derrick?"

His eyelids peeled back revealing bloodshot orbs of confusion. "What? Yeah, man. Derrick. How'd you know?"

She wrapped her hands around either side of his face, pulling back the skin at his eyes. "You listen to me and you listen close. If you so much as breathe a word about me, you even think about telling Derrick I was here, I'll find you. I'll hunt you like a dog. I'll wrench your guts out and cut them up for fish bait while you watch. You got me?"

He closed his eyes and nodded.

She shoved him and he slumped over on his side, gasping and moaning. She grabbed the baggie of pills, went straight to the dumpster at the back of the bar, and emptied it inside, shaking the tablets out of the baggie so they'd scatter in the greasy garbage. Then she tossed the one from her pocket in after them.

She came back and stood over Donny, staring for a moment. What should she do with this dumbass now? He had no idea where Flo was. He'd handed her off in The Bahamas and flew home without another thought about it.

Flo could be anywhere.

She kicked him in the side. *You dumb, worthless piece of crap. I ought to*—then she noticed something that made her smile. He was slumped over, passed out, on top of an ant hill. Fire ants. And they were already swarming across his cheek. She grinned all the way back to the Airbnb.

CHAPTER SIXTEEN

When Charity opened the door of the rental, Savannah jumped up from her chair, sending Charity's laptop bouncing across the carpet.

Charity came to a halt. "I'm sorry. I didn't mean to startle you."

"What did you find out? Did you find him? You've been gone so long. Does he know where my baby is?" She looked like she'd been mainlining coffee and hadn't showered in days.

"I found him." She dropped her tactical bag on the table. "It was Donny, for sure, who grabbed Flo. And he implicated Derrick. So, we have confirmation there."

She nodded but didn't seem relieved or surprised. She waited, eyebrows up. "But?"

"I'm sorry. He doesn't know where she is. Right after he grabbed her, he handed her off and flew right back here."

"Did you threaten him? Did you—" She shook her head, searching for ideas. "Did you—"

Charity touched her on the shoulder. "I did what I needed to do. And I'm convinced he doesn't know where she is."

Savannah slumped down on the couch.

"Now we focus on Derrick. We know for sure it was him. That's a big win. And like I said before, good news, really."

Savannah wasn't paying attention. Her eyes darted about and she chewed on her lip, as though she were trying to put together the pieces of a puzzle.

"What is it?" Charity asked.

"Annabelle."

"The wife." Charity sat down next to her. "What about her?"

"You told me to research Facebook."

Charity had forgotten about that. "And?"

"And my dirtbag ex-husband's new wife Annabelle has a profile." She got up, picked up the laptop, then sat back down with it on her lap and flipped it open. Her fingers moved across the mouse pad.

Charity gently took the laptop from her. "You don't have to show me. Just tell me what you found."

Savannah nodded, her eyes swirling about as she tried to formulate words. "Okay. I went back several years, to before she met Derrick. They had a really short courtship. Then they were married, all very quickly. At first, I thought she must've gotten pregnant. But then there was no mention of a baby. There was, however, a

span of time where she didn't post anything new, just shared sad memes. I think she had a miscarriage."

Charity was nodding. She had a feeling where this was going.

"Then all of a sudden, about five months ago, she's back posting happy stuff, cutesy posts."

"You think she got pregnant again?" Charity wanted her to sort it out and make a case by explaining it to someone else.

Savannah's eyes narrowed. "I think Derrick found out about Flo."

"Okay. What makes you think that?"

"I can't put my finger on it, but her posts...they aren't blatant, but she seems focused on older kids, not babies. The thing is, when you're pregnant, you think about the baby. Not older children. A precious, new little baby. And she's not."

"Okay, I'm with you. Derrick finds out Florence exists. His new wife wants a baby. So, he figures he can get back at you for leaving him and get his new wife the child she wants at the same time. Getting you sent to prison best suited his purpose for both. But how'd he get her to go along with it?"

"Oh, you don't know my husband. He's the master of twisting reality. Trust me. He probably gave her some long, detailed story about how I was always trouble, how he spent all his time keeping me in line, and now that he'd found out, through mutual friends, that I was running drugs, he'd have to save our daughter, the

daughter I had kept from him. He'd be the knight in shining armor and save her from me, the awful woman who'd tricked him so long ago."

She rolled her eyes. "Once, right before we got married, he found out about a guy in college who'd had a crush on me. The guy was harmless. I was nice to him. But when Derrick found out, he went nuts. He hunted him down, threatened the guy. At the time, he told me this whole, detailed story, about how he'd caught the guy looking in my window, then tracked him all the way across town. He had an answer for every point I asked. I realized, many years later, he was gaslighting me from the very beginning."

"I see your point."

She sighed. "I should have seen this coming."

"Okay, let's not go down that road. No should-haves. Let's stay focused on what we know now. Does she have any recent posts? Any hints where she is?"

"No. They stopped a week ago."

"So, maybe she's off the grid," Charity said. "Somewhere with no internet. Or Derrick warned her to stay off social media."

Charity got up from the couch and went to the window. She gazed outside, trying to get refocused with this new information. "Okay, let's walk back through it. Derrick learns about Flo. He wants revenge because you have kept her from him."

"Yes, it's all about me," Savannah said. "He's never forgiven me for leaving him. He doesn't care about Flo at all."

"But when you said he got a two-fer, I think you were on to something. Yes, his plan was to hurt you by kidnapping Flo and frame you for the drugs, out of revenge, sure. But, like you said, that makes it easy for him to get custody of Flo and give his new wife the child she's been wanting. He's put it all together."

Savannah was nodding. "That would be his kind of bat-shit crazy logic."

"From a legal perspective, he can argue it wasn't kidnapping, that you'd kept her from him, and he was concerned about her well-being. If his plan succeeded, and you were convicted of running drugs, the court would shrug. They wouldn't do a thing to him."

Savannah's face was turning red.

Charity kept on. "Until you're convicted, though, he'd want to keep her hidden. Since she's ten, she can talk." A light bulb came on. "That's why he had his thugs actually show her the bag of drugs on your boat. The proof. It was all for *Flo*."

Charity paused a moment, letting that sink in. "Having his thugs grab her from your boat in The Bahamas and plant the drugs was easy. Then he makes an anonymous call. The cops come and you're ranting about Flo, while they search the boat and find the drugs. Piece of cake. But convincing Flo, that's an entirely dif-

ferent thing. He needed her to believe you're a criminal and he's the good guy."

That made Savannah start to shake.

"I'm sorry. I shouldn't have said that."

"No, no. Go on. You have to be—just go on."

"All right." Charity needed to move to think. She paced across the carpet and back. "I bet that his men leaving you for dead wasn't the plan. Derrick is too smart to consider murder. Am I right?"

She nodded.

"So, right now, he's got to be worried that his guys killed you. He's got to come up with a new explanation as to how he got Flo."

A grin formed at the corner of Savannah's mouth.

"In this scenario," Charity said, "things don't look good for him. It puts him at the top of the suspect list for first-degree murder."

The grin turned into a genuine smile.

"But you're not dead. And either way, we'd have to prove all that in court."

"Well, what then?" Savannah said, the smile gone.

"There is no doubt in my mind now that Flo's with Annabelle." She would be stepping in to play the comforting mother, Charity was sure, but she couldn't say that out loud. "So, where are they? Trying to bring Flo into the U.S., even if they had her passport, would be risky. She has a different last name, and she's old enough to make a fuss. And transporting her somewhere else

would be risky too, for the same reason. The most logical plan would be to keep her in The Bahamas."

Savannah was nodding. It made sense to her, too. Then her mood changed, as though holding onto hope was too much. "The Bahamas is a pretty big place when you're trying to find one little girl."

"We'll find her."

Savannah nodded, but her head hung and the tears came again.

Charity sat down on the couch next to her, put her arm around her, and hugged her tight. "You're doing great. We're going to find her. We're so close. We're going to find her and then I'm going to take care of that turd-fondler ex-husband of yours."

Savannah pulled away from her, worry in her watery eyes. "What do you mean? What does that mean? You mean, kill him?"

Charity shrugged. The image of him hanging from a noose felt about right.

"No. You can't kill him." Suddenly, she had a surge of energy. "I mean, yeah, he's a dirtbag, and I hate him, but he thinks Flo's his daughter. That's not a capital offense. Punished, yeah. But dead? We can't. And you said yourself, he probably didn't want me killed either."

Charity stared into Savannah's eyes, then had to look away. The man did think Flo was his own daughter. Had she been too long in the mindset of eliminating the threat? And thinking that killing was always the answer? Had she seen too much bloodshed to be objec-

tive? The knot formed in her stomach again. How had she become so vengeful?

Savannah kept on. "I want him ruined. I want his reputation ruined. Drag him through the mud. That would be worse than death to Derrick. Make him suffer. Oh, man, if his dad disowned him, that would be a living hell. Bring it on. But we can't kill him."

"Okay," Charity said. "What do you want to do?

"I don't know." Now she got up and paced. "He's running drugs. We know that for sure, now, right? Can't we call an anonymous tip on him? Get *him* arrested?"

Charity pondered the implications. "We could. I guess. We could tail him, find out how he imports it, when he sells it, his schedule. We could do that."

Savannah stopped pacing and looked right at Charity.

In unison, the two said, "After we find Flo."

CHAPTER SEVENTEEN

Derrick sat at his big, wooden desk in his plush, executive chair, staring at the screen. He had to write a brief. He had to get it done tonight or his father would have his ass in a sling. The blank page stared back, bright white.

Maybe if he found some incentive. He clicked on the web browser and went to the page of a boat dealer down in Miami. He'd seen a boat in The Bahamas that he wanted. A sleek Cigarette boat, with bright orange and red stripes. Now that guy had some panache. Nobody thought that guy was a pussy. When he drove by, people turned and thought, *what a badass*. Derrick pictured himself behind the wheel, his hands on the throttles, a couple of topless babes on the bow. He'd get one of those battery-powered margarita makers and a wet bar. And down below, he'd make sure there were power outlets so the babes could keep their toys charged all the time.

He was going to have it, too. The kids at the high schools were going nuts for the pink bunnies, and Donny had just found someone at the college up in Charleston

to move more. He couldn't supply them fast enough. He had to rethink his business structure, though. Donny was too much of a meathead to run things. He needed someone with some brains. Maybe Ben. Nah. He wasn't that bright either. Why was he always having to deal with losers? Couldn't anyone think for themselves anymore? Swimp would have been perfect. Not overly bright, but smarter than Donny and Ben put together. And he was huge. But the dumbass had gone and got himself killed several years ago.

He'd have to figure it out. And then the money would be flowing and he'd be like El Dorado, covered in gold. He'd be bathing in it.

All he had to do was figure out this Savannah debacle. What the hell had his boys been thinking? He shuddered. They weren't supposed to kill her. Jesus, what was he going to do now? He had to find a way to explain how he had Florence. He could say that he'd confronted Savannah about her criminal behavior the day before, and she'd agreed to let him take Florence for a while, until she got her act together. Then he didn't hear from her at all. He'd say it was her drug-running that caught up with her. *Gee, officer, I'm heartbroken to hear about her death. Such a waste. She had so much potential and wasted it with her nefarious ways.*

Yeah, that would work. He loved the word *nefarious*.

There it was, the boat, in full technicolor, right there on the page. Stripes weren't enough, though. Blazes of fire. That's what he wanted. Fire streaking down the

sides. So, when he went flying by, people would turn their heads to look and say, *now that guy's a badass.*

Derrick poked around, looking for a price. Why didn't they just post the damned price? Why did he have to go on some kind of twisted Easter egg hunt to find out anything? It made his head hurt.

He glanced at the clock on the wall. It was nearly eight p.m. Another kicker would get him through the rest of the night. He picked up his briefcase and opened it on the desk. He had a small stash in there, just enough that wouldn't cause any questions if someone went snooping. He popped one into his mouth, downed the last of his coffee, and snapped the briefcase shut.

"Tiffany!"

His assistant scurried into his office. "Yessir?"

Tiffany stayed until he left, regardless of how late. That's what law clerks did. But why did she always look like a scared little bunny?

"I need you to whip up a rough draft of that brief for me."

"Yessir."

"I'm swamped with other stuff. Have it to me within the hour?"

"Yessir." She nodded.

Was that all she ever said? He stared at her a moment, thinking about it. Yep. He was sure of it. That's all she ever said. He waved a hand at her. "Go on, now."

"Yessir." She spun on her heel and scurried back out the door. *Go on, little bunny.*

He wondered for a moment if he could get away with putting her over his desk and having his way with her, but she'd probably mutter *yessir, yessir,* the whole time, driving him nuts.

Why didn't women have backbones? Like Chandra. And Savannah.

He picked up the baseball that sat on the edge of his desk, a ball he'd caught when his father had taken him to a game when he was seven. He hated baseball, but his dad had saved that damned ball and Derrick had to keep it on his desk like it was some kind of trophy.

He pushed his chair back, squeezing the ball in his hand, then spun around and stared at the fat goldfish in the bowl on his filing cabinet. Did they leave Savannah floating face-down in the water? *Animals.*

How'd that happen anyway? Savannah was a strong swimmer. She'd always been in the water. Since they were kids. He took the key from his pocket, unlocked the top drawer of his desk, and pulled it open. He kept a picture of Savannah stashed there. She stared up at him with that beautiful smile. Why'd she have to die? The bitch was supposed to go to prison. Not die. Those fuckups. He was gonna cut their balls off.

He swung back around, squeezing the baseball tighter. The rage surged up, out of nowhere, and he threw the ball, knocking the fishbowl from the cabinet. It shattered and water splashed everywhere. He leapt from his chair. "Tiffany!"

She rushed in. "Yessir? Are you all right, sir?"

"Dammit, clean this up. I told you I didn't want a damned fish."

"Yessir. Right away, sir."

She bent over to try to catch the flopping fish. He liked that.

His phone buzzed. He checked the caller ID. Anna. Didn't she ever quit? "What now?" he said by way of answering, his eyes still on Tiffany's ass.

"What did you do?" Her voice was shrill and accusatory. How dare she?

"What are you talking about?" He went down the hall and out the door. Fresh air. That's what he needed. A little fresh air.

"Tell me what's going on. Right this instant. Florence said she saw her mom killed. Is that true? What did you do? Is she dead? What happened, Derrick?"

Pain exploded inside his skull. Why did he always have a throbbing headache? Maybe because she never shut up. "I told you. I found out she was running drugs and I had to get my daughter away from her right way. You know how the judicial system is. It could have been months and months. You have to trust me."

"You're not answering my question. You always do this. I ask a question and you deflect. I want a straight answer, Derrick."

God, she sounded just like Savannah. Why had he gotten married again? He rubbed his temples. Just a few more minutes and that kicker would kick in. He smirked. That was amusing, *the kicker would kick in.*

"Derrick! Are you listening to me?"

"Yes, dear."

"Don't you *yes dear* me. I need you back here. I don't know what to do. Florence is adamant that her mother is dead, that those men you sent killed her. I don't know what to tell her."

"Tell her whatever you want."

"That's not an answer."

"You know how it is, Annabelle—how you get wound up sometimes and you can't think clearly? All these things going on at once. I know how stressful it can be. But you need to find a way to relax. I thought the islands would be good for you. Isn't the house nice?"

He hit the button on his key fob to unlock the door of his car. God, he loved the sound of that chirp. It was the sound of money.

"This isn't about me." Her voice was like an ice pick in his ear. "Don't you dare make this about me."

"I tell you what," he said, trying to think. He had to divert her. What would she want? What was she always asking for? "When this is all over, we'll take a vacation. Together. Isn't that what you're always harping at me to do?"

"Harping?"

He cringed. Wrong word. "We'll go to Hawaii, or Cabo, or see the Grand Canyon. Whatever you want. We'll take two weeks. Isn't that what you're always asking for? Two weeks. Together. The three of us. You start planning it and that's what we'll do."

"I don't want a vacation. I want the truth, Derrick. What happened to her mom?"

He huffed. "Fine." She was like a dog with a bone. "She got rough, fought with my men. I don't know." The pounding in his head was getting worse, like a whore with some kind of jackhammer fetish was trapped inside his skull and couldn't get off.

"What does that even mean?"

"They had to get out quick, to make sure to keep the girl safe."

There was silence. Blessed silence. Though now he could hear the echo of the jackhammer, like it was at the end of a long, hollow tunnel.

"Oh my God, Derrick."

He pulled the phone away from his ear. Why was it so loud all of a sudden? "What?"

"They didn't tell you. They killed her. Florence said they left her, floating face-down in the water. If she wasn't already dead, she must have surely drowned." She drew in a sharp breath. "That's murder. Derrick, you're an accessory to murder."

"No, no. That's not—you need to stop listening to a child. You're overreacting, as usual."

"Oh, Derrick, what are we going to do?"

He sat down in the driver's seat of his car, held the phone to his ear with his shoulder, and rubbed his temples with both hands. "You're not going to do anything. I have everything under control. I'm the one who's calm, here. You're freaking out over nothing. It's

hearsay. From the mouth of a kid, no less. Do you see what I mean? You're unstable. You've gotten yourself into a tizzy over nothing. The overactive imagination of a child."

Silence again. Oh, how he loved silence.

"But what if it's true?"

"It's not."

"But what if it is?"

"God, you're like a broken record. Don't you listen to me?" He couldn't take any more of this crap. "Listen, I gotta go."

"Don't you dare hang up on me."

He stabbed *End* and slammed the phone down on the dash.

One more kicker. That would do the trick. One more. Then his head would be fine.

CHAPTER EIGHTEEN

Flo waited, patiently, like her mom had taught her to do when fishing. You couldn't force a fish to take the bait. You had to dangle it in front of them and wait. Flo didn't have any bait, but she knew about waiting for the right moment.

She paced around her room, thinking through the details. Now she had a plan A and a plan B. Just like Charity had told her. A backup plan, she'd called it. Plan A was to get the phone and call her mom. Since she didn't know the password, she'd have to get it right after Anna used it, so it would still be on and not need the password. But how long before it would shut off? She didn't know. She'd have to wait and see.

When nighttime finally came, she'd put on the ridiculous pajamas Anna had given her. They had little hearts all over them. That was for little kids. But she didn't say anything. She crawled into bed and pretended to be asleep when Anna checked on her.

As soon as she left the doorway and headed downstairs, Flo got up and sneaked down the hall to the top

of the stairs. Anna was talking on her phone out on the porch. Flo couldn't tell what she was saying, but she sounded mad. Who was she talking to? Derrick? He was probably mean to her, too.

Flo went down one step, then another. She couldn't hear the words, but it didn't matter. She was on the phone. That's what Flo wanted.

The sliding door slammed shut. Flo peeked. Anna went right to the couch, still on the phone. "Don't you dare hang up on me," she said. She yanked the phone from her ear and stared at it. The clock was now ticking until the phone locked up. This was Flo's chance. She flew down the stairs and jumped onto the couch next to Anna. "There's something outside. I heard it. Something out there. I'm scared."

"I'm sure it's just the wind, dear," Anna said, setting the phone down on the end table.

How much time did she have? "No, it was someone outside. I know it."

"I'm sure it was just your imagination, dear."

"No, it's not. And I can't sleep now. There's someone out there."

Anna was getting agitated. "I don't know what you want me to do."

"Go check. Make them go away. I'm scared." *Just leave your phone.* "I think they're outside my window."

"No one's outside your window."

"They are. And they're trying to come in."

Anna got that exasperated look on her face again.

"Please, I can't sleep." Flo moved to her lap and pressed her into a hug. "Please!"

"Oh, all right. I'll go check, if it'll make you feel better." She got up. Flo grabbed her hand, as though needing to hold it. That way, she couldn't pick up the phone. "Stay inside. I'm sure it's nothing, but I'll go check."

"Thank you."

As soon as Anna was out the door, Flo grabbed the phone. It was still on. A rush of excitement surged through her. She punched in her mother's phone number and hit send. It went right to voicemail. Why wasn't her mom waiting for her to call? It took forever to get through the message. Anna was going to be right back. Finally, it beeped. "Mom, Mom," she cried. "I'm in a white house on Lubber's Quarters, right across from Tahiti Beach with someone named Anna. Please come get me. Please." She disconnected. Anna would be right back. She couldn't get caught. She looked up. Anna was still outside.

She quickly searched her mom's name in the web browser. Nothing came up. She tried, *Savannah Richmond death*. Nothing. If her mom had died, there'd be a report. Something. She was sure of it.

The back door opened.

Flo quickly set the phone back down. Wait, had it been face-up or face down? She couldn't remember. What if Anna figured out what she'd done?

Anna sat down on the couch beside her. "There's nothing outside, dear. Like I said, it was your imagination."

She tried to get her arm around Flo, but Flo squirmed free. As she pulled away, she put her hand on the edge of the table, on the phone, and knocked it to the floor.

"What is wrong with you?" Anna said, her voice stern. "What is all this about?"

Flo stood up and faced her. "I guess getting kidnapped has me all upset."

Anna rose from the couch. "Now you listen to me. I won't have that kind of talk. Your father explained all that. You can't stay with your mom because she's going to jail." Her face changed. "Honey, listen to me. I know this is hard. But your mom has been breaking the law. She's been selling drugs."

Flo shook her head. "No, she hasn't. You're lying."

"I'm not lying. The police found drugs on your boat."

"They put them there. I saw them. They came on board and held my mom down and then took something from their pockets and said they found it in the drawer. But I know it wasn't there. They were lying."

"I know it seems—"

"No, you don't. You weren't there. You don't know my mom."

"I'm not sure you know your mom either. Sometimes we love someone so much, we can't see the truth. Especially if they've been lying to us on purpose."

"My mom doesn't lie to me. And she's not selling drugs. She wouldn't do that."

"Really? Derrick told me that—"

"Maybe Derrick's lying. Did you ever think of that?"

Her neck started to turn red. "You watch your mouth, young lady."

"Sometimes we love someone so much, we can't see the truth." Flo threw her own words back at her. "Especially if they've been lying to us on purpose."

Anna's face went white. The redness in her neck spread up to her cheeks while she stared at Flo. "You shut your mouth."

"Make me!"

Anna lunged at her. She ducked and ran around to the other side of the couch.

"He's a liar and you know it. He's a mean, nasty liar."

"You go to bed right this instant."

"He's not my father and you're not my mother."

Anna faltered. Her lip quivered and her eyelids blinked a couple times, like she was trying to get control of herself. "I know you're upset now. It will take some time, but you'll see. You'll see that I love you and you'll love me like your mother."

"You're wacko, lady. I hate you. You'll never be like my mom."

"You go back to bed right now." Anna spoke through clenched teeth, her hands on her hips. "You go back to bed and you get down on your knees and you thank God that you've got me to take care of you. Because your

no-good mom is a deadbeat loser who's going to jail. Do you hear me? She's going to jail and you're staying right here. And you're going to learn to like it. And tomorrow, we are going to build a sandcastle. Together. You and me. Like mothers and daughters do. Do you understand me?"

Anna fought back tears, staring at Flo.

"Fine." Flo said. "I'll go back to bed. But you can dream all you want. You'll never be my mom."

She padded back up the stairs. *Always have a Plan B.*

CHAPTER NINETEEN

After Charity insisted that Savannah take a quick shower, they left the B & B, headed back to the airport, and were back in the air within the hour, headed straight for Marsh Harbor. Since the trip was a hundred miles or so shorter, fuel wouldn't be a problem—even with an easterly wind, which would make it a bumpy ride, and burn more fuel. Charity wasn't going to let anything slow them down.

Twelve miles out over the ocean, Chyrel phoned. Charity patched the call through their headphones.

"Hey, wanted you to know right away, I got a ping on an alert I set up. Derrick was on a flight this morning. He's entered The Bahamas."

Donny had just flown out of the Marsh Harbor airport, on his way back to Beaufort. "At Marsh Harbor?" Charity asked.

"You got it."

Charity and Savannah exchanged a nod of confirmation.

"We think Flo's still there," Charity said. "What time does the flight land?"

"One hour."

"I won't make it in time to follow him from the airport. But my money's on him going to check on Flo and Annabelle."

"I was thinking the same thing," Chyrel said. "As soon as I saw where he was headed, I started poking around. He flies to The Bahamas pretty regularly, about once a month. He was there when Flo was kidnapped."

Charity and Savannah shared a glance.

"I'm sorry. I should've checked that before."

"It's okay," Charity said. "But once a month, huh? Now we can be pretty sure his source for the drugs is in The Bahamas."

"I can't find any record of where he stays," Chyrel went on. "When he goes, it's almost always for an overnight. He's either paying cash or has some other arrangement. I'll keep digging. But that's not all I've found. I went over his checking account and found a check that cleared four months ago through a Bahamian bank. It was made out to a Rudy Larrea."

Charity looked to Savannah. She shook her head. She didn't know him.

"I searched his name," Chyrel went on. "He owns five rental houses in the Abaco islands. I'm thinking—"

"Flo's in one of them," Charity said, sure of it.

"I'm sending the coordinates of the five houses now. Good luck."

When Charity disconnected the call, Savannah reached over, took her hand and squeezed. Charity smiled. "We're going to get her."

Big tears streamed down Savannah's cheeks. Happy tears. Tears of hope. Flo was in one of those five houses. She had to be.

When Chyrel's email came through with the information on the five houses, Charity had Savannah find each one and mark their GPS locations on the Navionics app on her phone.

"There's one on Great Abaco Island, right in Marsh Harbor," Savannah said.

Charity shook her head. "I doubt Derrick would choose that one. He'd want the house to be more remote. Save it for last."

"I agree," Savannah said. "Like you said, Flo's old enough to make a fuss. He wouldn't want a neighbor to see or hear anything."

"Okay, so we start with the other four."

"There're two on Green Turtle Cay, one on Great Guana, and another on Lubber's Quarters."

"Which one do you want to start with?"

"What do you think?" Savannah said.

"Those islands are miles apart. We can hit the two right away on Green Turtle, if we land at Treasure Cay International. Fifty percent. Let's start there and work our way south. We'll need a boat. "

"Okay," Savannah agreed.

Charity called Henry. He answered right away.

"We're flying back to Abaco right now. We think Flo is being held in a rental house there, one of five owned by a Rudy Larrea. We don't know which one and they're scattered on different islands. You wouldn't know him by chance, would you?"

"No, I'm sorry, I don't."

"All right. I'll land at Treasure Cay airport in—" she checked the instruments "—three hours. Can you have your man meet us at the ferry dock? The one with the fast boat?"

"Done."

"Thanks, Henry." She reached for the button to disconnect. Savannah chimed in. "How's Woden? Is everything okay with him?"

"Well, he chewed a beach chair to bits, has dug about twelve holes, and eats more than a teenage boy."

Savannah grinned. "Yep, he's acting like himself. Sorry for the damages."

"Not a problem, it was old and rotten. He just turned it into kindling for me."

"Thank Angelique for us again," Charity said.

"Will do," he said, and the line went dead.

Savannah bounced in her seat, all nerves and pent up energy. Charity knew how it felt. She, too, was a bundle of nerves, the knot in her stomach pulsing now with her heartbeat. In the past, whenever she was headed into a fight, she got a little anxious. Mainly, she'd learned to channel those feelings into a sharp focus. But this was different. This was Flo. She couldn't fail.

Three hours later, right on schedule, they landed at the Treasure Cay airport. Savannah and Charity paced in tandem as they waited for the customs agent. As soon as Charity signed the documents to leave her helicopter and have it fueled, the agent arrived. One thing Charity loved about The Bahamas—no questions asked. Just a warm welcome.

Once they were cleared, Charity said to Savannah. "I need to get something from the helicopter. It will just take a second."

Charity hurried to her helo, popped the latch for the secret compartment, stuffed some tools, coiled zip-ties, and other assorted items she might need into her tactical bag, and tucked her Colt in at her back.

When she got back to Savannah, they sprinted toward the ferry dock. As Henry had promised, their driver was already there, in the bright red and yellow-striped Cigarette boat.

As they boarded, Charity shook the driver's hand and looked him right in the eyes. "I'm sorry. Please forgive me. When you drove us before—well, it was quite an emotional morning. I never asked your name."

The young man grinned. "All is forgiven. I am Edwardo."

"Nice to meet you Edwardo. Here's the plan." She explained how they were going to check two different houses on Green Turtle Cay and she needed him to find a dock or anchorage down the shoreline of each one

so they could approach them on foot, without causing suspicion.

He nodded in understanding.

"Fantastic. Let's go."

Savannah and Charity helped him cast off the lines as the engines sputtered to life, belting out their distinctive high-performance exhaust notes.

Once they were past the mouth of the marina area, he thrust the dual throttles forward and Charity felt the rumble in her whole body as she was pushed backward in her seat. The boat surged through the water and up on plane, hitting top speed within seconds. She wasn't usually a fan of go-fast boats, but today, she wanted all that horsepower and more. It could suck all that gas, scream that obnoxious noise, leave a wake a mile high. She didn't care. Just get her where she needed to go to find their girl.

They covered the distance in minutes. The first house was along the shoreline on the north end of the island. They did a quick pass by it and saw no one outside, which wasn't surprising. It was off season. The house had pink siding, a white metal, A-frame-style roof and a row of palm trees along the southern border of the lot.

Edwardo did as Charity had asked and found a dock just south of there. It was at a private house, but no one seemed to be home there either.

"I have a phone," Edwardo said. "Call me so dat I know your number and if you need me, I will be right dere."

He gave Charity the number and she entered it, touching *Talk*. When Edwardo's phone rang, she touched *End* and pocketed her phone.

He pulled up and they jumped off. He said he'd wait offshore, watching for any boat traffic and would be right there when he saw them return.

"Remember," Charity said to Savannah as she moved down the dock and up a set of stone stairs, "stay behind me. I know you're wound up, but we don't want to tip them off. Okay? Promise me."

Savannah mumbled something.

Charity came to a halt and spun around. "I'm not messing around. Look me in the eyes. Promise me you'll do exactly as I tell you."

Savannah nodded. "I trust you. I promise."

Satisfied, Charity continued down the side of the house and out to the road behind. They'd go along the neighboring house's drive and cut through the property. From the water, she'd noted the house next door had yellow siding and thicker foliage along its southern side. As they came upon it, Charity held up her hand, indicating to Savannah to halt and wait. With a quick glance over her shoulder, Charity confirmed Savannah had stopped. Good. She gestured for her to stay put. She wanted to check for occupancy at the neighbor's house first.

There was no car in the drive, but that meant nothing. There weren't any on Green Turtle Cay; only golf carts. There wasn't a golf cart there either. She eased around

the corner of the house and crept up to the first window. No one was in that part of the house. She went to the next window. No one there. Finally, she made her way to the screened porch overlooking the sea. It was empty.

She jogged back to get Savannah, who, thankfully, had waited where Charity had left her.

"C'mon. The coast is clear."

They crept along the backside of the neighbor's house to the rear of the pink-sided house. Charity checked once again to confirm it was the right one. Palm trees lined the south side of the lot. This was it. She took the Colt from her waistband and held it firmly in her right hand as she sprinted between the houses. Once she'd reached the exterior wall, she turned so her back was against it, since she wanted to check inside the windows there before going around to the front. With Savannah inching along behind her, she side-stepped to the first window, carefully placing each foot to avoid the ornamental cactus planted there. No one was inside. At the next window, still no one. Stealthily, she pressed forward, moving toward the screened porch. It was empty, too. She'd have to go inside.

She gestured for Savannah to wait where she was and moved to test the door lock. As she did, a man's voice came from the direction of the water. She spun around, holding the Colt behind her back. A man dressed in wet swim trunks and flip-flops, carrying a can of beer, climbed the stairs toward her. "Hello there. Can I help you?" His voice revealed his uneasiness.

He wasn't Derrick. That's all that mattered. Charity quickly tucked her Colt under her shirt and called out. "Oh hello. I'm sorry, I didn't realize anyone was here. The Realtor didn't mention it. We're just looking to buy in this area, and I was told this house is for sale. Are you the owner?"

He seemed to readily accept her explanation and relax. "No. Just renting for the week. I didn't realize it was for sale, though."

"Well, what do you think? Are you enjoying the place?"

"Oh, sure. Except for the sunburn." He grinned and gestured toward the door. "Did you want to take a look inside?"

"Oh no, no. Thanks so much. Don't let me bother you. Like I said, I didn't realize it was currently occupied. I can come back anytime." She quickly retreated, waving and smiling.

As she came around the corner of the house, she gave Savannah a nod to follow. Once they were back on the road, she said, "One down. Four to go."

The next house was on the south side of the island. Edwardo picked them up and they did the same routine with that house. It was empty. No sign of anyone.

"We've got three more," Charity told Savannah. "Don't get discouraged."

House three was on Great Guana Cay, close to Nipper's Beach Bar & Grill. It sat up on a high bluff, overlooking the Atlantic to the east. There would be no docks or

places to anchor. They'd have to approach on foot from the west.

Edwardo brought the boat in to shore at Grabbers Bed, Bar & Grill, the other party spot on the small island, and Charity and Savannah crawled out onto the bow and hopped off onto the sandy beach. Music blared from the speakers around the tiny pool. Three people sat at the bar and a drunk guy in bare feet stood at a post, tossing a ring attached to a string, trying to get it to stay on a hook. Typical island fun.

Charity and Savannah strolled through without notice.

The house was less than a mile down the narrow street, then one block up onto the bluff.

When they arrived near the house, Charity led once again, Savannah staying three paces behind, obeying all her signals. But this house proved to be another dead end. A nice family of four from New Jersey had been there for ten days. They didn't like the noise from Nipper's, but other than that, it was paradise, according to them.

Back to the boat they went.

"I still think the one in Marsh Harbor is the least likely. That leaves the one on Lubber's Quarters," Charity said to Savannah.

She agreed. "It's getting close to sunset, though."

"All the better." Charity turned to Edwardo. "So, put the hammer down."

CHAPTER TWENTY

As Derrick's plane touched down in Marsh Harbor, he felt an overwhelming pressure in his brain, like his head was in a vice that was being twisted, notch by notch. Annabelle was in a panic. Why couldn't she just be happy? He'd given her what she wanted, and at great risk.

Women. Now, he'd had to lie to his father to leave the office once again, a day after he'd gotten back, telling him Annabelle was sick and he needed to check on her. He wasn't sure how long he could keep this up.

Of course, his dad had suggested that he nail her while he was there. Get that little grandson of his in the oven.

A stop by Chandra's place was what he needed. Nothing made him relax like that woman. One hour in her bedroom and he'd be a new man. Besides, she'd texted, saying she needed to talk to him about a shipment. He hoped it wasn't held up. The college up in Charleston would be good for thousands of bunnies. It seemed like some sick, latent-childhood-psychosis-thing

to him, like mommy didn't love them enough to give them their Flintstone vitamins, but what did he care? He'd raised the price and was selling even more. Dumb bastards. *Retirement, here I come.*

At least Randall was right on time, waiting at the airport in his black, four-door plain sedan. What was it anyway? A Taurus? Derrick crawled into the backseat. It reeked of cologne and cheap air freshener. "Hey, man, when are you going to get a new ride?"

Randall didn't respond. He shifted into drive and pulled away from the curb.

"Dude, you need something with a little more style." He leaned forward to push his head between the seats. "Something that'll attract the ladies."

Randall turned to look at him directly. "I'm married."

"What? You never told me that." *Married? What the hell?*

"You never asked, sir."

Never asked? Derrick flopped back into the seat. *Dumb bastard.*

"Where to today?" Randall asked.

"You know where." He was pissed. Now he'd have to get a new driver. Married guys didn't know where to find the ladies.

When he pulled up to Chandra's house and Derrick got out, Randall stepped from the car. "About what time will you be calling for me to pick you up?"

"I won't," Derrick said over his shoulder as he walked toward the house.

He flung open the screen door and went inside. Chandra was in the kitchen, stirring something on the stove. She wore jeans and a blue cotton top that was a few sizes too small. He liked the way the thin fabric stretched across her oversized breasts. He liked that skimpy red lace thing she wore last time even better.

"What are you doing? Why are you dressed? I texted to let you know I was coming." He frowned as she continued stirring without acknowledging him. "Well, woman? I've only got an hour. Get your ass into the bedroom. Get into that red lacy getup. I like that one."

She turned to face him and gave him that look. Something was up.

"C'mon baby." He moved toward her. "I need some lovin'. I feel like my head's in a vice. It's a whole-bottle-of-lube kinda day."

She dropped the spoon in the pot. "We need to talk."

The vice tightened. "Dammit!" He slammed his fist down on the counter. "What the hell do we need to talk about? We don't talk. We screw. That's what we do."

"Not today."

Anger surged through his veins. How dare she? He had a mind to grab her by the arm and drag her into the bedroom. Instead, he plopped down in one of the chairs at the tiny kitchen table. "What, then?"

A metal travel case was on the table. She flipped it open. It was stuffed full of the green baggies loaded with little pink pills.

"Is there a problem with the bunnies?"

"No. That's what you ordered, and since you already paid for it, there it is. But that's your last shipment."

He came up out of the chair. "What the hell are you talking about? Those are selling like crazy. We've damned near doubled the numbers."

She shrugged, then flipped her hair back as she often did.

"Well, can you still get the greenies?"

"Listen," she said, with that stern look she got when she was about to rip his shirt off. His thoughts went back to the bottle of lube. "Sit down." She gestured toward the chair. He plopped back down. "We got a problem. You're reckless. That shit you pulled with the woman and the girl? You need to think. That was some risky shit."

She sounded just like his father. He clenched his teeth together, trying to stay calm. "Why's that any of your business anyway?"

"It's all my business. I don't want nothing ever coming back to me."

"It won't."

"Yeah? How do I know that?"

He rose and put his hands on her shoulders. "I will always protect you. Nothing's going to happen."

She threw her hands up, shoving his hands from her shoulders. "Don't treat me like I'm some delicate flower you can sweet-talk into your bed. This is business, Derrick."

He could feel his neck turning red, which made him even more angry. "What are you even talking about,

anyway? My daughter has nothing to do with our business together."

"Oh, really? Who'd you hire to go with your man to grab her? Huh? Those were my soldiers."

"Well, yeah, but it was a side gig. They weren't busy and—"

She crossed her arms in front of her chest and scowled at him like his black Gullah nanny had, when he was little. Her index finger came up and she shook it at him. "Nope. I didn't sign up to be involved in no murder."

Derrick winced. "Hey, that was their fuck-up. I didn't tell anybody to murder her. That's not on my hands."

"It don't matter. From now on, you get your supply somewhere else."

"What!" Derrick huffed. From the look on her face, he knew she wasn't going to back down. She wasn't going to put that red lacy thing on either. *Dammit!*

He had to give it one more try. "C'mon, baby. You know how good we are together. Let's get naked and I'll show you how sorry I am."

"Oh, you're sorry all right. Take your case and go."

He stared. Was she for real? "I can't take that case. How the hell am I supposed to get it into the U.S.?"

"Not my problem." She turned her back on him and picked up the spoon again.

"You bitch!" He grabbed her by the arm.

"Now that ain't the way to talk to a lady." Her arm came around and she smacked him in the face with

the spoon. Stew splattered across his face and down his shirt.

"What the hell!"

The spoon came down on the top of his head. "Get out!"

"Screw you." He backed away from the crazy woman, grabbed the metal case, and stormed out the door. The midday sun hit him as if he'd stepped in front of a blast furnace. How people lived here, he didn't know. He was going to buy a little log cabin in the mountains, where it snowed half the year. He'd chop firewood, and hunt for his dinner. And he'd have none of this crap to deal with. At his cabin, there'd be no women allowed. Especially women with spoons.

He took his phone from his pocket and started to dial Randall. Then he remembered that S.O.B. was a liar, so he walked down the sidewalk toward town, where he could hail a taxi. He'd find a new driver. Someone who was actually loyal. He was done with getting jerked around. In fact, screw that. He'd rent a skiff. He could drive himself out to the island. What'd he need a driver for anyway?

He got on the phone and made the arrangements. A skiff would be at Witch Point for him, the key under the seat. He found a taxi—a plain white car—and headed for Witch Point.

When the taxi dropped him off, it was already nearly dark, but he could see the skiff, right where it was sup-

posed to be, pulled up on shore. "See that?" he said to the driver. "That's what power gets you."

The taxi driver stared. The dumb bastard had no idea what he was talking about.

"Who cares?" Derrick said, turning away. "Whatever."

The skiff was a plain white, sixteen-foot, center-console boat. "What is it around here?" he said to no one. "Doesn't anyone have any style? Vanilla-land, I swear."

The key was under the seat. He dropped his case on the floor and fired up the engine, then pushed the boat from shore and managed to flop over the bow into the boat without getting his shoes wet. He drove the rented skiff full throttle across the water, from Witch Point to the rental house on Lubber's Quarters Cay.

CHAPTER TWENTY-ONE

The rental they were looking for on Lubber's Quarters Cay was a large, gleaming white chalet across from the well-known Tahiti Beach on Elbow Cay. It was built into the hillside, with a large water view deck spanning the whole front. There were two sets of French doors and a big sliding door in the center. A steep staircase led from the dock up to the porch. Scrub brush and small cactus grew all around the structure. If Charity and Savannah were to approach from the water, they'd have to walk right up those stairs, so they'd have to find a way in from behind.

"It's so pretentious," Savannah said, as they cruised past. "So totally Derrick."

"Why don't you pull up to Cracker P's," Charity suggested to Edwardo. "No one will think twice about us walking through."

Cracker P's Bar & Grill was a world-famous party spot about a half mile to the south. Tourists came for the full-moon beach parties, where the crowds danced all night drinking Cracker P's signature drink, The Shotgun, and

got rowdier and rowdier as the night wore on. Most of the customers didn't realize that the property was over seven acres and spanned the island, beach to beach. Behind the bar, nature trails wound through the lush forest. Lubber's Quarters had no roads north of Cracker P's, so Charity was confident they'd find a walking trail that led all the way to the back of the rental house.

Edwardo tied up at the dock and agreed to wait there. Eighties music blasted from speakers mounted on palm trees that swayed over some twenty-somethings in bikinis playing beach volleyball, the version where one held a drink in one hand and hit the ball with the other, while giggling and bouncing. Charity got the sense Edwardo had the patience to wait all night.

"Keep your phone close to you," Charity said to Edwardo. He nodded, but his eyes never left the game.

The sun would be setting within the hour. Charity wanted to get through the woods before nightfall. She headed toward shore, Savannah right behind her.

On the foot of the dock stood one of those signposts covered in driftwood markers pointing in different directions, each with a town's name scrawled across it in bright paint, and the distance in miles.

Just point me toward Flo, Charity thought as she passed. She walked along the north wall of the main building, away from the beach, past the sapodilla trees the legendary Cracker Pinder had planted, and found the trail that led into the woods.

She set a good pace. Dusk brought out the mosquitoes and she didn't want to be wandering around in the dark, guessing at different paths. Savannah simply followed and said nothing, but Charity felt the vibe of anticipation. This was the house. She knew it. They'd find Flo and this would all be over.

Looking up to the treetops to gauge the direction of the sunlight, she chose the trail that would take them north.

"What are you going to do when we get there?" Savannah asked.

"I'm going to assess the situation. Then I'll decide."

"But what if—"

Charity came to a halt and spun to face Savannah. "We're not going to do this. We're not going to play the 'what if' game. We're going to get to the house, assess the situation, then act accordingly. Do you understand?"

"Yes, but—"

"But nothing. Listen, I don't mean any disrespect. I can't imagine what it feels like to be in your shoes, but we have to be smart about this. For all we know, Derrick could have that house surrounded with armed goons. I'm not going to be taking any chances."

Savannah clamped her jaw shut and nodded.

Charity continued on. The house was about half a mile north. As she walked, she counted her paces. When she estimated they were close, the trail split in two directions. They took the path to the right, back toward shore.

As they crept along, they scanned the woods for any sign of guards but saw nothing. And when they came upon the house, the windows glowed with light. Dusk had settled into darkness.

Charity eased along the side of the house, her Colt in her hand, while Savannah continued to follow. The windows on this house were too high off the ground to see in, so she'd have to sneak onto the porch. As they moved toward the seaward side of the house, Charity heard a skiff approaching out front. The engine quieted and the boat slowed in the water. It was heading for the dock. She motioned for Savannah to halt and stay put. Charity inched forward, leaning against the wall at the corner of the house, where she could see part of the dock.

Whoever was in the skiff wasn't very skilled with a boat. He rammed the dock, bounced off, then had to toss a line to lasso the post. Once he had it tied up, the driver, visible by the accent lights only from the waist down, stomped up the stairs. He carried a large metal case in his hand. The man looked like Derrick, but she wasn't sure.

"Annabelle!" he yelled.

Charity swung around to check Savannah's reaction. Her eyes were wide, her whole body erect. She nodded up and down. It was Derrick.

"Annabelle. I'm here."

A blond woman came out onto the porch. She was model-thin with perfectly coifed hair. Flo wasn't with her.

"I didn't know you were coming back so soon." Her voice sounded like syrup.

"Isn't that what you asked me to do, sweetheart?"

Charity turned to check on Savannah again and bumped into her. She'd moved up to look over Charity's shoulder.

"Where's Flo?" she whispered.

Charity shook her head. "We need to wait—"

"Wait for what?"

"For confirmation she's here. Just try to relax."

"What's in that briefcase?" Annabelle asked.

"Nothing. Don't worry about it." He went into the house and Annabelle followed. He said something else, but Charity couldn't make it out.

She turned to Savannah. "I need you to stay here. Do you understand? Promise me you'll stay put."

Savannah nodded, but Charity didn't feel especially confident. There was something about the way she shifted from one foot to the other. But she promised.

Hidden by the darkness, Charity slipped onto the porch, crept to the edge of the window and peeked inside. Derrick and Annabelle were in the kitchen, talking in whispered tones—a further confirmation for Charity that Flo was likely in the house and they didn't want her to hear.

Behind her, she heard footsteps and spun around. Savannah crossed the porch in an instant and barged through the door. "Derrick, you son of a bitch!"

Oh shit! Charity rushed in behind her, her Colt trained on Derrick.

"Where is she? Where is she!" Savannah shouted, her voice shrill with desperation.

"You're alive?" Derrick said, his mouth open. "You crazy bitch!"

Annabelle gripped Derrick by the arm, hiding behind him. "What's going on, Derrick? Who is she?" Her eyes were locked onto Charity and the gun she held.

Charity calmly stepped forward, holding her weapon steady, making clear she'd be asking the questions. "Where's Flo?"

Annabelle stared, frozen with fright, her tiny hand gripping the strand of pearls at her neck.

Charity raised the gun a little higher. "Where is she?"

The poor woman managed to raise her index finger and point toward the stairs.

Savannah launched in that direction.

"Wait!" Charity said, stopping her. She spun around. "I want them to go first." She gestured with the gun for Derrick and Annabelle to lead the way up the stairs.

Savannah looked like a greyhound, stuck behind the starting gate.

As Derrick passed by her, she sneered at him. "You're going to rot in hell for this, you son of a bitch."

He sneered at her. "Yeah? Been running drugs much?"

"Oh, do you mean the drugs found on my boat? Yeah, that was long after I'd reported it stolen, so—" She held up her hands and shrugged.

"Hold on just a second," Charity said. "What's in the case?" She didn't need any surprises.

Derrick scowled.

She waved the gun. "Put it on the counter. Slowly."

Grudgingly, he picked up the metal case and set it on the kitchen counter.

"Turn it toward me," Charity ordered.

Derrick slowly turned the case, his eyes darting to his wife.

"Reach over and open it," Charity said, raising her weapon and pointing it directly at the man's chest. "I don't need to remind you how slowly you want to do that."

Derrick cautiously reached over and popped it open. The case was stuffed with green plastic bags sealed with yellow tape. Through the plastic Charity could see the same pink bunny pills Donny had been selling. Ecstasy.

Derrick snarled at Savannah. "You had no right to keep her from me."

"Who are you kidding? Is this some kind of show for your new wifey? You don't give a shit about Flo."

"Get moving," Charity said, nudging Derrick along.

He and Annabelle climbed the stairs and moved toward a bedroom door. Derrick pushed it open, looked around. He turned back to Annabelle. "Where is she?"

Annabelle pushed past him. "She was just here a few minutes ago," she said, panic in her voice.

Savannah drew in a sharp breath. She rushed into the room, spun around, and cried, "She's not here."

Charity forced Derrick and Annabelle into the center of the room, trying to keep calm, but she was shaking. Her stomach had dropped to her knees. Where was Flo? Had they set up some kind of bait and switch? She lifted the Colt, aimed it right between Derrick's eyes. "Where is she?"

"How the hell should I know?" He jerked his thumb toward his wife. "She was supposed to be watching her."

Annabelle looked grief-stricken. "Well, I... she was here, I swear it."

"Look," Savannah said. She approached the open window. A bed sheet was tied to the window crank and draped outside. She leaned out and yelled, "Flo! Flo! It's your mom. Flo!"

Charity sighed, overcome with relief as she lowered her weapon, but still held it ready in both hands. *I'll be damned. That spunky little girl got away.*

"It's all your fault," Derrick grumbled at Savannah. "You did this, you bitch. She wouldn't have run away if she knew I was really her father."

Savannah spun around, her eyes on fire. "That's the funny thing about all this," she said, and surged toward him, stopping within inches of his face. "She's not even yours."

With a swift motion, she kneed him in the groin. As he doubled over, she clenched her fists together and hammered the base of his skull, dropping him like a stone.

Charity grinned. Her only regret was she couldn't see his expression when Savannah had dropped that bomb.

Savannah went right back to the open window and yelled for Flo.

Charity pulled two zip-ties from her tactical bag and handed them to Savannah. "Know what to do with these?"

Savannah started for the door, ignoring Charity, who kept her weapon trained on the wife as she blocked Savannah. The woman's eyes were on fire.

"Savannah, wait. I need you to focus for one more minute. We can't just leave these two and dash off after her yet."

Savannah looked down at Derrick. His new wife simply stood where she'd been, head down, completely deflated at the realization of what her new husband had done.

Charity shook the zip-ties in Savannah's face. She took them and threaded one into a loop before pulling Derrick's hands behind his back and cinching it tight.

"His legs, too," Charity instructed.

Savannah stood over him after binding his ankles. "What about her?" she asked, pointing at the wife.

"Get down on your belly next to him," Charity ordered Annabelle. She complied without hesitation. Charity

took two more zip-ties from her bag and Savannah bound the wife's hands behind her back as Charity secured her feet. They weren't going anywhere.

"Where could she have gone?" Savannah asked, frantic.

"We didn't pass her on the trail. Maybe she went down by the water?"

In a flash, Savannah was out the door, running down the stairs and out the front door, yelling Flo's name.

Charity caught up with her on the porch. "Stop. Stop. Wait. Take a moment to think." Charity grabbed her by the shoulders. "We have no idea how long she's been gone. Where would she go?" Savannah started to cry, shaking her head. "Listen to me. You know her. If she was lost, where would she go? What have you taught her? I'm sure you planned for a time she might get lost, right?"

She nodded, pulling herself together, thinking. "I've always said, if we get separated, go to someone you know, or..."

"Or what?" Charity wanted to shake it out of her, but she had to be the calm one.

Savannah's eyes snapped up, locked with Charity's. "Or to a busy place, with lots of people. That's always safest."

Charity looked out at the water and the porch lights, scattered among the trees on Elbow Cay across the channel. To the north, around the famous lighthouse,

the sky glowed from the lights below. “She’s swimming to Hope Town.”

“Oh my God. It’s nighttime. The boats go racing through here at night. Oh my God. Oh my God!”

Charity wasn’t listening. She was already rushing down the stairs to the skiff.

CHAPTER TWENTY-TWO

Flo swam hard. She had to get to shore, get to Hope Town. There were lots of people there. Someone would help her find a policeman and they'd find her mom. But she didn't realize it was going to be so far. She was getting tired from swimming, and the boats scared her when they zoomed by. It was like they didn't even know she was there.

She didn't like swimming in the dark. She'd gone for a dip with her mom at night many times, but her mom wasn't here now. She was all alone. And there were sharks. When she swam with her mom near Tahiti Beach, they'd seen a reef shark. A pretty big one. And that was close by.

But she couldn't go back. She had to keep swimming. Keep swimming.

At least in the dark, Anna wouldn't be able to see her. She probably didn't even know she was gone yet. It had been so easy to crawl out the window and down to the ground. Anna'd been crying on the couch when Flo left.

Maybe she'd cry all night and wouldn't even notice she'd escaped.

Anna was sure to check on her at some point, though. Probably when she went to bed. Then what would she do? She didn't have a boat to come after her. Unless her jerk husband came back. Did he mean it when he said he'd hit her with his belt? She didn't want to find out.

Flo kept swimming. She'd make it, she knew she would. Charity had told her to keep her head down, stay focused. She could do that. But she was getting tired and her legs were numb. She'd put on that stupid swimsuit that Anna had bought her. It was too tight. She didn't have a choice, though. She couldn't swim in her clothes or those dumb pajamas.

She stopped paddling to check her progress. She'd been swimming forever and she wasn't even halfway. Or was she? How far was it? She couldn't tell in the dark. She had headed toward the lighthouse. The beacon swung around every fifteen seconds, guiding her along the way. But she wasn't getting any closer. It was still so far.

She was so tired. She wanted to cry, but she couldn't swim when she was crying. And she couldn't go back. She had to keep swimming; she didn't want to drown. So, she put her head down in the water and kicked her feet. Her arms felt all googly, but she had to go on. She tried to do everything Charity had taught her, but it was hard to keep going.

From behind her, she heard another boat, only this one sounded like it was really close. She kicked hard, digging in with her arms. She had to get out of the way.

The boat got closer. It had a spotlight shining on her. They'd found her! They'd take her back. *No, no!* She had to get away.

Under water. Dolphin kick. Like Charity had taught her. That's what she needed to do. As fast as she could swim. She drew in a deep breath and went under. With her hands above her head, cutting through the water like a rocket, she kicked with her feet pulled together. She could do it. Just a little farther. If she could get to shore, she could run.

But she had to come up for air. She sucked in a big breath and went down again. The whir of the engine was so loud, so close, and the spotlight lit up the water around her.

No! No! She had to get to shore. She had to find her mom. She couldn't go back.

CHAPTER TWENTY-THREE

With Savannah in the bow, shouting like a mad woman, Charity had pulled the skiff away from the dock. She didn't know what Flo would do, head straight for Tahiti Beach on Elbow Cay, then walk to Hope Town, or try to swim all the way to Hope Town, which was a very long way for a little girl to swim. But did Flo know that?

Under the seat, Charity had found a spotlight and handed it to Savannah.

Savannah flicked it on and scanned the water ahead, calling Flo's name over and over.

Charity had no idea how long it had been since Flo had left. She could be close to shore or nearly to the other side. Or maybe they'd missed her on the trail and she was on the island, running toward Cracker P's. But her gut told her Flo was in the water.

The channel along this section was about one mile wide. She had decided it was best to start a crisscross pattern, covering as much area as possible within the

reach of the spotlight. She headed northeast, toward Hope Town.

When they saw nothing for some distance, she turned back southeast. Maybe Flo had realized it was too far to swim to the lighthouse and headed straight across the bay to Tahiti Beach. There was no compass on the skiff, so she estimated her course and kept the boat at high idle speed.

After five minutes, they'd seen nothing. She turned to the northeast again and held back the urge to push the throttle down. If they were going to find her, they had to use a logical search pattern and keep a steady pace.

But how long could Flo swim without tiring to the point of exhaustion? Would she panic? That was how people drowned. Even people who knew how to swim. If she'd been in the water for a while now, she could be getting cold. And there was some wave action in this channel. Would the waves bother her if some crashed over her head?

Don't go there, she told herself.

Savannah's voice had risen an octave higher since they'd left the dock.

"We'll find her," Charity said, as much to herself as Savannah. "We need to stay calm, keep our heads. If she's out here, we'll find her."

Another skiff went zooming by, full throttle, no running lights on. Charity wanted to chase the man down and shake him. Didn't he know how dangerous that was?

"There!" Savannah shouted, pointing. "There's something in the water. It's someone swimming. It's her! Oh my God! It's her!" She held the light on the figure in the water, but it submerged.

Charity didn't get a good look at it. "Are you sure it wasn't a dolphin?"

"It was her. Flo! Flo!" Savannah was on the verge of losing it.

The state of mind Savannah was in, it likely was a dolphin. But wishful thinking wouldn't change a dolphin into Flo. Charity tried to remember how long Flo had been able to hold her breath. Was she trying to stay under, away from the boats? Or was it a dolphin?

The thing popped to the surface. It her! It was Flo! She sucked in air and submerged again.

Charity turned the wheel.

"It's me, Flo! It's your mom! Florence!"

Flo probably couldn't hear her mom over the engine. Charity brought the skiff right up beside her, threw it in neutral, and killed the engine.

"Flo! Flo! It's mom!"

Flo popped up, wiped her eyes, and looked at the boat. Savannah flipped the light around, holding it so Flo could see her. The girl burst into tears, crying so hard Charity was afraid she'd start gulping water and drown. She fired the engine back up and nudged closer, her hands shaking.

Savannah leaned over the side, her head jerking back and forth. "Where'd she go? Where'd she go?"

"Did she go under?" Charity's heart went into overdrive, her pulse throbbing in her throat. She couldn't engage the engine. What if Flo was under the boat?

Savannah cried out. She had Flo by the elbows. She lifted her out of the water and fell back into the skiff, her arms wrapped around her daughter, crying as hard as Flo was.

Charity held her hand to her mouth, eyes wide. She was so overwhelmed. With trembling knees, she collapsed into the driver's seat. All the fears, all the stress she'd been holding in seemed to seep out of her pores at once and she suddenly felt more exhausted than she'd ever been in her whole life. But she managed to push off her seat and went to them, wrapped her arms around them both, and cried. Never had she felt such sweet relief. They'd found her.

They'd found her.

CHAPTER TWENTY-FOUR

Charity hated to cut the reunion short but sitting in a tiny skiff in the middle of that busy waterway in the dark wasn't prudent. Besides, she still had to deal with Derrick.

She shifted the boat into gear and headed back to the dock. A plan was already forming in her mind.

"Why are we back here?" Flo asked. "I don't want to go back."

"It's okay," Charity said. "Nobody is going to hurt you here now."

Flo looked up at the house, uncertain.

"It's all right, honey," Savannah said.

"We won't be here long," Charity said. "I promise. I'll go first, okay?" She stepped out of the skiff. She needed to make sure her captives hadn't made a miraculous escape.

Once Flo seemed all right, Charity climbed the stairs to the bedroom where she'd left Derrick and Annabelle bound. They were still there, lying on their bellies. As

soon as she entered the room, Derrick started spewing a barrage of angry words in no particular order.

She went to the window, took hold of the bed sheet Flo had used to escape, tore off a corner, and shoved it into his mouth.

As she glanced at Annabelle, she'd have sworn she saw relief on the woman's face. Derrick really was a piece of work.

"What were you thinking when you married that man?" Charity said.

It was a rhetorical question. Annabelle closed her eyes and looked as if she were praying.

"I've got some planning to do," Charity said. "So, you just sit tight." She noticed Flo's clothes in a pile on the floor and picked them up.

Annabelle's eyelids sprang open. They were red from crying. "Please. Please don't leave me here like this."

"But who's going to keep him company?" she said over her shoulder as she walked out the door.

Back downstairs, Flo and Savannah were seated on the porch in one of the white rattan chairs. Savannah had found a blanket and had wrapped Flo like a burrito. While Savannah rocked her daughter, Flo was talking up a storm.

"Annabelle was okay, I guess. She made me grilled cheese sandwiches. But she's a little crazy, I think. That man was so horrible, though! I hate him! He said he was my dad. But I knew he wasn't."

Savannah rocked and rocked, tears streaming down her cheeks.

"I knew you weren't dead. I knew it," Flo went on.

"It was Charity. She saved me," Savannah said, her voice a whisper.

Flo grinned. "Just like you told me! She's our guardian angel."

Charity's knees suddenly buckled and her pulse fluttered. She gripped the doorframe to keep herself from crumpling, then managed the two steps to sit down in a chair. Finally, she drew in a long, deep breath, trying to get her heart rate back under control.

Savannah nodded. "Thank you. Thank you, Charity. I don't even know how to—" she puffed, needing air "—to ever thank you."

Charity shook her head. She didn't have words.

"And I'm sorry," Savannah continued. "I just couldn't help myself and barged right in."

Savannah opened her arms. Charity rose from the chair and into her embrace, with Flo squeezed between them. She pressed her lips against Flo's wet hair.

"Thank God you're all right," Charity breathed. When she finally felt calmer, she pulled away. She couldn't let her emotions get the best of her when there were still things to do, so she summoned her naturally tactical-oriented thinking process to again take over. Soon, she knew exactly what her next steps should be.

"I have some things to finish here," she said to Savannah, gesturing with her head toward the upstairs bedroom.

Savannah nodded in agreement, though her eyes revealed she was wondering what Charity planned to do.

"Don't worry," Charity said with a wink. "I have a plan. For what you wanted."

She took her cell phone from her pocket and called Edwardo, giving him the green light to come pick them up.

"When he gets here, I want you to take Flo to the boat, take her down below, and keep her warm. Understand?" She handed her Flo's clothes.

Savannah nodded, taking the clothes from her. She clearly knew what Charity was trying to say—keep her from seeing anything. She lifted Flo from her lap, took her by the hand, and headed toward the dock.

"Aren't you coming?" Flo asked.

"I'll be right behind you," she said. "I'm going to make sure they are long gone and can never find you again. Sound good?"

Flo nodded. "But Charity? Don't hurt them."

Charity gave Flo a long, assessing look. For all Derrick had put the girl through, Flo held firmly to her sweet nature.

The metal case still lay open on the kitchen counter. Charity searched under the sink and found a pair of rubber gloves. After pulling them on, she located a cleaning rag in a drawer and stuffed it into her pocket.

Then she broke open one of the baggies, pocketed three of the pink pills, grabbed a glass from the cupboard, and filled it with water at the sink. Satisfied that she was ready, she headed up the stairs.

"Please don't hurt me," Annabelle whined as she entered the room.

"I'm not going to hurt you. But the thing is, I don't know what you know or don't know, or how you were involved in this kidnapping," Charity said to her, "and I don't care. You married this dumbass. Your fate's tied to his."

She grabbed Annabelle by the shoulders, sat her upright, crammed one of the pink bunny pills into her mouth, and told her to swallow. The woman froze. She didn't want to. Charity reached to the back of her waist for the Colt. "Are you afraid to take what your husband has been peddling to kids?"

Annabelle's eyes flitted to Derrick and back to Charity, and then her expression slowly dissolved into surrender. If she didn't know what Derrick had been up to, she did now.

Charity didn't get the gun halfway around her hip before Annabelle swallowed hard. Charity took hold of her hair with her left hand and tipped her head back. After shoving the Colt back into her pant waist, she held the glass of water to the woman's mouth and poured. Annabelle glugged down a swallow full.

Next, Charity sat Derrick upright. "Guess what? You get two."

He glared at her. He'd already spit the sheet out of his mouth. "You foul bitch."

She shrugged. "That all you've got? I've been called worse. Of course, that's usually right before I put a bullet between someone's eyes."

That got his attention.

"That's right. You messed with the wrong woman. By the way, I met your pet, Donny. I didn't even have to ask. One of these pink bunnies and he was singing like a little bird about how he'd grabbed Flo for you. You really should hire better help. Someone who has an actual set of balls."

Derrick narrowed his eyes. "You bitch."

"That's right. Though I've got a lot of nicknames. There's the one I have for my interrogation techniques." She leaned down and whispered, "That one's not nice to repeat in mixed company, though."

Spreading one hand wide, she clamped it over his nose, pushed his head back, and then pried his jaw open with the other, which held the two remaining pills pinched between her thumb and forefinger.

"I used to have to do this with my dog," she said. "Easy-peasy, right down the hatch." She shoved the pills to the back of his throat. He gagged and clamped down on her gloved fingers. "Atta boy." She slid her hand out of the glove and rammed his mouth shut, then held her hand over his nose until he started to turn red.

"Just swallow already." He finally had to. She let go and he spit and sputtered. "Wow, you're such a wimp."

She kicked him in the side. "Now get up." He squirmed. "Oh, right. You're hobbled."

Pulling a heavy knife from her back pocket, she flicked the blade open to the locked position. With a flash of steel, the zip-tie parted from Annabelle's ankles, then Derrick's. She picked up the glove he'd spit out and put it back on, then pocketed the cut zip-ties.

"We're going for a ride," she said, bringing out the Colt once more. Before leaving the room, Charity wiped clean the windowsill where Savannah had leaned out the window calling for Flo.

At the front door, Charity used the rag in her pocket to wipe the doorknob. As they made their way down the stairs to the living room, Charity glanced out the window and saw that Edwardo had arrived at the dock.

"Move," she told Derrick and Annabelle, gesturing toward the porch. With her gloved left hand, she took the opened baggie from the case and tossed it on the countertop. With his check for the rental, it would be another obvious dot for the cops to connect. She snapped the metal case shut, took it by the handle, and followed them out.

"Get in the skiff," she ordered, once they were on the dock. They willingly did as she demanded. The ecstasy must have been kicking in.

Edwardo stood in the cockpit of his boat and gave her a nod, confirming Savannah and Flo were on board.

"Do you have a tow line?" she asked him.

He nodded and went to a stern lazarette, flipped the top open, and rummaged around inside.

Charity got into the skiff and tucked the metal case against the captain's chair, where she zip-tied it to the base. Another zip-tie went through the locking mechanism. Without a knife, Derrick wouldn't be able to get it open or throw it overboard. She removed the access panel to the gas tank and, using her knife, cut the rubber hose that fed gas to the engine.

Edwardo climbed out of his boat and onto the dock. "I've got the line."

"Tie it to the bow cleat," she said. "We're going to tow them out to the middle."

He did as she asked, then got back into his boat and fired up his engines.

"I'll stay in the skiff with them for now. Tow us out, then I'll get into your boat."

He nodded.

As he moved the Cigarette boat away from the dock, the slack came out of the tow line, and Charity shoved off from the dock. The skiff spun around and was pulled by the big boat.

As Edwardo drove toward the open water, the little skiff pitched and rolled on the waves.

Annabelle had begun to coo and giggle. From the look on her face, Charity assumed she was enjoying the experience.

"You like those pink pills, huh?" Charity said, shaking her head. The woman's mascara had run down her

cheeks and her hair was mussed. "Wish I had a mirror. It'd really make your day."

Annabelle's eyebrows went up. "Really?"

"Really." Charity grinned. Poor woman.

Once they were in the middle of the channel and Edwardo had pulled back on the throttle, the big boat settled in the water. Charity called Chyrel and quickly gave her the news that they'd found Flo.

"Thank God," Chyrel said, genuine relief in her voice.

"I'll fill you in on the details later, but right now I need another favor."

"Name it."

"Make an anonymous call to the Bahamian Defence Force. You've seen someone in a white, twenty-foot skiff acting strangely." She gave her the location. "You're sure they're on drugs, whatever, make it sound urgent. They can catch them right now."

"Got it. I'm dialing already." She disconnected.

Charity gestured to Edwardo that she was ready. Edwardo grabbed the tow line and, hand over hand, brought the skiff up to his boat.

Before Charity stepped from the skiff, she clipped the zip-ties from Annabelle and Derrick's wrists. Neither cared. They were lost in an ecstasy high. The way she'd secured the metal case, they wouldn't be able to ditch the drugs. They were sitting ducks for the police to pick up.

Charity climbed aboard the Cigarette boat. "Let's move away, but not far," she told Edwardo. "I don't want them out of my sight until the cops get here."

Fifteen minutes later, the police arrived in one of their 41-foot SAFE Boats—an Offshore Interceptor—lights flashing. The spotlight went on, lighting up the skiff with Derrick and Annabelle aboard.

The police boarded the tiny vessel, and within moments had the two in handcuffs.

Charity watched through Edwardo's binoculars, smiling, as the police took possession of the metal case.

In the past, she would have put Derrick in the ground without another thought. But Savannah was right—he didn't deserve to die. Sure, he was a dirtbag drug dealer who'd kidnapped Flo, but he genuinely believed she was his daughter. This way, he'd get the justice he deserved. Who knew? Maybe for him, it would be worse than death.

Savannah had been right about another thing: watching him being taken away in handcuffs was pretty damned gratifying.

CHAPTER TWENTY-FIVE

As Edwardo headed toward Andros, Charity slipped down below. Flo lay in Savannah's arms sound asleep. Savannah's eyes were closed, but Charity wasn't sure if she was asleep. She didn't want to disturb them, so she sat down across from them and simply enjoyed the moment. They were reunited. A few days ago, she wasn't sure if that would happen.

A warm tingling started through Charity's body. She'd had a lot of missions, but none were as satisfying as this one. Maybe she wasn't meant to be a mother herself. Maybe, instead, she'd been meant to be here, in this moment, to save this little girl from harm. Perhaps everything before now, every bit of training, every mission she'd done, had led up to this moment. If that were true, she was fine with it. That instant, when Savannah had pulled Flo out of the water, when she was safely back in her mother's arms, was worth everything. She felt tears warm her eyes again.

Charity laid her head back. Exhaustion overcame her and she was soon fast asleep.

They arrived on Andros just after dawn. As they idled toward the dock, they could hear Woden barking. Before Edwardo had the boat tied up, the dog came running down the dock as though he knew Flo was aboard. Maybe he did.

Savannah lifted Flo from the boat onto the dock. She was forced to sit down on the dock while Woden plastered her with dog kisses and she giggled with delight.

As Savannah and Charity disembarked and walked down the dock toward shore, Henry and Angelique were heading out to greet them.

"Ah, so all is well," Henry said, smiling.

Charity gave him a hug. She hadn't been much of a hugger before, but right now, it felt good, natural. She squeezed him tight.

"Well, well," he said, grinning.

She hugged Angelique, too. The way she hugged her back, Charity knew she understood how she was feeling. "Thanks for everything," Charity said.

"Are you kidding? We paced a lot, that's all we did. And prayed, of course."

"You were here for me—that's what mattered."

"Indeed," Angelique said with a knowing smile. "Now, let me make you breakfast. I'll have it done in a jiffy. Pancakes and eggs. All the fixings."

"That sounds wonderful."

Angelique disappeared into her cabin.

"What next?" Henry asked.

"Well, we need to get Savannah's boat. It's been impounded. I'll get my chopper back down here, then get back to *Wind Dancer* and—" she shrugged "—life can get back to normal." As she said it, she knew it would never be normal again. Those few minutes when she was in the water, swimming toward *Sea Biscuit*, while that skiff was driving away with Flo, had changed her. She'd never felt so vulnerable, so helpless. Not when her father had died. Not in Afghanistan, when she was shot down. Not anytime during her captivity there. Never.

"Well, anything you need, you let me know." Henry patted her arm.

Charity's eyes were on Flo. She'd run down the dock with Woden and was now throwing a ball for him. Savannah was right beside her.

"I'm sure Savannah won't be able to leave her side for some time."

"Would you?" Henry said.

"Probably not ever," Charity admitted.

"That's the thing about raising kids, though," he said. "From the time they're born, a parent's job is to help them grow away, to face life on their own. And all you want to do is protect them from it. That's why it's the hardest job in the world."

Charity looked up at him and smiled. "My dad told me almost the exact same thing once."

Henry walked the length of the dock with her, then left her with her feelings.

Killing people had been easy, Charity thought. Helping them grow, well, that was an entirely different thing. She moved to stand beside Savannah, who was watching Flo romp and play with Woden.

"I don't envy you having to explain all this to her," she said.

"Yeah," Savannah replied. "It's my fault. I'll start with that."

"Don't be so hard on yourself. That was one hundred percent Derrick's doing."

"Yeah, well."

"She's going to be okay." That made Savannah's eyes pinch closed as she held back tears. Charity placed her hand on Savannah's shoulder. "She's all right. We found her. She's safe now."

Savannah pulled herself together. "Thanks to you."

"We did it together."

Savannah nodded.

"So, what do you plan to do about Jesse? Are you going to tell him?"

Her head swiveled toward Charity. "What do you mean? Why should I tell him?"

"It will get back to him. And the thing is—" Charity paused, thinking. Maybe she shouldn't tell her. No, after all that had happened, she needed to know. "Jesse knows he is Flo's father. Over a year ago, you were in Cane

Garden Bay and he saw you. He took a water bottle that Flo had used and got it tested for DNA. It was a match."

Savannah simply looked away. She must've suspected all along. Flo didn't look like Derrick. She had Jesse's fair hair and blue eyes.

"So, he's known, but yet he didn't..." she said. A whisper.

"He did, actually. Even before he found out. He'd been looking everywhere for you. But when he found you, you were with another man. I think he figured it was better to leave well enough alone."

"Yes." Savannah nodded, her eyes on Flo. "Well enough alone."

"He's done what he thought was best. He set up a trust fund in Flo's name, with you as executor, in case anything happens to him." She hesitated. "I thought you should know."

Charity felt uncomfortable then. It wasn't her secret to tell, and yet she had. She hoped it was the right thing.

Savannah nodded but turned away.

Henry approached with a cell phone in his hand. "I forgot," he said, handing it to Savannah. "Chyrel sent this for you. She said yours was damaged."

"Thanks, Henry," Savannah said, taking the phone. "I guess I'll have to put all my contacts in this new one."

"If I know Chyrel," Charity began, "that phone will have the same number and all your contacts will be there."

"She can do that?"

"I've found that there isn't much that woman can't do, when it comes to electronics."

Savannah turned the phone on, then looked up in surprise. "I have a message."

She clicked for it to play on speaker. Flo's voice came on. "Mom, Mom," she cried. "I'm in a white house on Lubber's Quarters, right across from Tahiti Beach with someone named Anna. Please come get me. Please."

Savannah wobbled. Charity grabbed her by the arm. "She's all right."

Flo turned when she heard her own voice.

"You called? And I...my phone, it was in the water."

"It's okay, Mom. I had a plan B." She turned and ran after Woden, skipping along the grass.

Charity grinned and Savannah burst into tears. The phone in her hand rang. She looked up as though she didn't know what to do. "It's my mom."

"Answer it," Charity said.

Savannah clicked to answer and held the phone to her ear. "Hello?" She listened. "Yes, Mom. I just got my phone and—no, I don't know anything about that." She held the phone out in front of her and turned it to speaker.

"Well, I got a call this morning from the Beaufort Gazette. Apparently, that no-good ex-husband of yours has been dealing drugs. Can you believe that? He was caught in The Bahamas. He and that new wife of his. I knew she was no good. The paper wanted a quote from me, but I don't know what to say. I called Loretta at my

sewing group. Everyone here is already talking about it. Loretta said that Betsy said that Gloria was in earlier, all upset. Seems old Harry Coleman is fit to be tied.

"Apparently, Derrick called in the middle of the night asking him for bail in The Bahamas. You know what he told him? He said he didn't have a son. His name has already been stripped off the door at the office. Knowing old Harry, I kinda feel sorry for Derrick."

"Yeah, me too, Mom," Savannah said. "Me too."

She grinned at Charity and Charity grinned back.

"I gotta go, Mom. Love you. I'll call you back later." She disconnected.

It's funny, Charity thought, how differently lives can end up after one simple decision, or one simple event. Whatever had made Derrick decide to kidnap Flo had set those wheels in motion. He had been so sure he could frame Savannah with the drugs and now, he'd be the one facing true justice.

Then there were the other occasions, other small incidents that led people down different paths. What would have happened if, when Jesse found Savannah at Cane Garden Bay, she'd been alone? Or she'd never met Jesse in the first place? Or never gone back to Derrick afterward?

And what about her own life? If her mom hadn't left when she was a child? Or if her dad were still alive? What would her life have been like then? Would she have joined the military? Would she be married, with 2.3 kids of her own?

Flo ran toward her, holding Woden's ball out for Charity to take. "Come play with us, Charity."

"I'd love to," she said, letting her thoughts drift away. All that mattered right now was that little girl's smile.

THE END

KIM'S AFTERWORD

When Wayne first invited me to co-write a Charity book, I wasn't sure. Often, working with another person can be difficult. But as we talked, the ideas started flowing and when I realized how much fun we were having, I was all in. Charity is a very different character than Poppy McVie (from my own book series), who wears her heart on her sleeve, yet Wayne was determined to dig deeper, to find Charity's humanity, to get her to open her heart. In the end, that's what I wanted, too. I hope you've enjoyed her journey.

– Kimberli

OTHER BOOKS BY KIMBERLI A. BINDSCHATEL

The Poppy McVie Adventure Mystery Series

Operation Tropical Affair
Operation Orca Rescue
Operation Grizzly Camp
Operation Turtle Ransom
Operation Arctic Deception
Operation Dolphin Spirit
Operation Wolf Pack

If you'd like to learn more about Kimberli's Poppy McVie series, Saving Animals One Adventure Story at a Time, find her at

WWW.POPPYMCVIE.COM

OTHER BOOKS BY WAYNE STINNETT

The Charity Styles Caribbean Thriller Series

Merciless Charity
Ruthless Charity
Reckless Charity
Enduring Charity
Vigilant Charity

The Jesse McDermitt Caribbean Adventure Series

Fallen Out
Fallen Palm
Fallen Hunter
Fallen Pride
Fallen Mangrove
Fallen King
Fallen Honor
Fallen Tide
Fallen Angel
Fallen Hero
Rising Storm
Rising Fury
Rising Force
Rising Charity
Rising Water

If you'd like to receive Wayne's newsletter,
please sign up on his website:

WWW.WAYNESTINNETT.COM

Every two weeks, he'll bring you insights into his private life and writing habits, with updates on what he's working on, special deals he's heard about, and new books by other authors that he's reading.

Made in the USA
Columbia, SC
23 January 2024

30840823R00143